Russia

Turkey

CASPIAN SEA

DYAAR

GOLNAZ

TEHRAN

SHAHREZA

Iraq

P E

Kuwait

Saudi Arabia

PERSIAN G

ISFAHAN

BAFT

Afghanistan

PERSIA

Pakistan

PERSEPOLIS

GULF OF OMAN

ALSO BY NOOSHIE MOTAREF

Tapestries of the Heart

LAND OF ROSES
and
NIGHTINGALES

Seven Adventures of a Persian Girl

Translation and Adaptation
by Nooshie Motaref, Ph.D.

Illustrated by David E. S. Anderson

A3D Impressions
Tucson | Minneapolis

A3D Impressions™

A Division of Awareness3D, LLC
P.O. Box 57415
Tucson, AZ 85735
www.a3dimpressions.com

First A3D Impressions Edition 2018

Library of Congress Cataloging-in-Publication Data

Names: Motaref, Nooshie, author.
Title: Land of roses and nightingales: seven adventures of a Persian girl / translation and adaptation by Nooshie Motaref, PhD; illustrated by David E. S. Anderson.
Description: Includes bibliographical references. | Tucson, AZ: A3D Impressions, 2018.
Identifiers: ISBN 978-1-7320677-1-4 (Hardcover) | 978-1-7320677-0-7 (ebook) | LCCN 2018935968
Subjects: LCSH Fairy tales—Iran. | Tales—Iran. | Women—Folklore. | Women—Iran—Folklore. | BISAC
Classification: LCC GR290 .M67 2018 | DDC 398.2/0955--dc23

Book design by Richard G. Wamer, JR
Art Direction by Donn Poll
Illustrations by David E. S. Anderson

Library of Congress Control Number: 2018935968

ISBN 978-1-7320677-1-4
ISBN 978-1-7320677-0-7 (eBook)

1 2 3 4 5 6 7 8 9 10

ACKNOWLEDGEMENTS

I greatly appreciate everyone on my team whose aid was instrumental to get this book into the hands of our readers, specifically young adults and educators.

In particular, I am deeply indebted to my long time friend and muse, Lauri Burke. Her undying enthusiasm and interest in the Persian culture have been an inspirational path throughout the years in my life since I came to this country.

My thanks are also due to Ron Lancaster, my storyteller coach. His immense patience for listening to me to convert these stories into the style of oral tradition is commended. In addition, Glenda Bonin, the president of the Tellers of Tales Tucson, deserves my gratitude for her immense encouragement in these fables.

Of utmost importance in supporting this project is Dr. Karen Zittleman, the author of *Still Failing at Fairness: How Gender Bias Cheats Girls and Boys in School and What We Can Do About It*. It is an honor and privilege to have her expertise in academic writing. Her insight to move this project has been outstanding. In addition, professor Colleen Cosgrove's speciality in higher education has given this book distinctive direction.

I wish to express my deepest gratitude to all the talented members of A3D Impressions publisher, specifically Rick Wamer. His tireless attention to details and producing a lovely book cannot be missed. Moreover, the illustrator, David Anderson, with his artistic expertise breathed a new life into these stories.

My perpetual gratitude goes to all my friends and family who have supported me in every aspect of my life.

Thank you!

Land of Roses and Nightingales
Seven Adventures of a Persian Girl

Table of Contents

LAND OF ROSES
and
NIGHTINGALES

Seven Adventures of a Persian Girl

With
Literary Analysis, References, and Reader's Guide

INTRODUCTION

Having grown up in Persia, my veins carry the oral tradition of storytelling as vital as life's blood. As a little girl, I loved the summer nights when my grandmother and I would move our mattresses outside. Laying down, we gazed at a sky filled with stars. Listening to her stories of "Aladdin's Wonderful Lamp," "Ali-Baba and the Forty Thieves," or "The Seven Voyages of Sinbad," was a delight. I recall also being fascinated by a teller of tales, *dervish*, who enacted epics from *The Book of Kings (Shahnameth)* in our streets or teahouses. At age five I sat in the first row, enthralled by the dervish, an old man dressed in a wool garment, playacting the legends. I could drift easily into his stories. His sharp hand-clapping interrupted my fantasies — an unsettling experience. These tales strengthened my imagination. The stories convinced me that anything is possible if I rely on myself using my mind and my heart as my guides.

In the spirit of Scheherazade, the main character and the storyteller in *One Thousand and One Nights*, I invite you to unfold these seven adventures of a Persian woman. Each journey is based on Persian fairytales and folktales written in the style of the oral tradition of storytelling. These fables have trickled down from the ancient times when the Persian Empire was at its utmost power and the country was the beacon of the world. In essence, the female character in these stories is a spirit who travels through different times in the country. Known by Westerners as Persia and by its natives as Iran, it is named after their race, Aryan. Each fable starts with the main character who is also its narrator claiming, *"I don't know if you believe in reincarnation, but I do because I have been reincarnated as a Persian girl many times, I re-*

member, once…". According to some experts, the ancient Aryans believed in reincarnation as part of their monotheistic religion, Zoroastrianism. Reading these stories is a journey much like a magic carpet ride.

My major goal in translating these tales is to provide our young generation with the tools to depend on their own wits, bravery and resilience. Furthermore, my intention is to provide professors, teachers, librarians and storytellers these fables for their classrooms to further their students' comprehension of archetypes in the Persian culture. I sincerely believe these tales offer a unique and fascinating glimpse into a past culture, opening a bridge to better understanding and closing the cultural gap—an important objective in today's fractured world.

It is imperative for all generations to realize that regardless of where we started from, the bottom line is that we are all part of humankind.

The title, *Land of Roses and Nightingales*, refers to Persia. It is said that in the eighteenth century when western scholars arrived, they called it the Land of Roses and Nightingales because of its beautiful rose gardens with chirping of nightingales serenading them.

Enjoy these adventures as they transport you to those rose gardens of the past.

Author's note: Please see the literary analysis interpretation of each story based on Carl Jung's theory—Collective Unconscious, and Reader's Guide at the end.

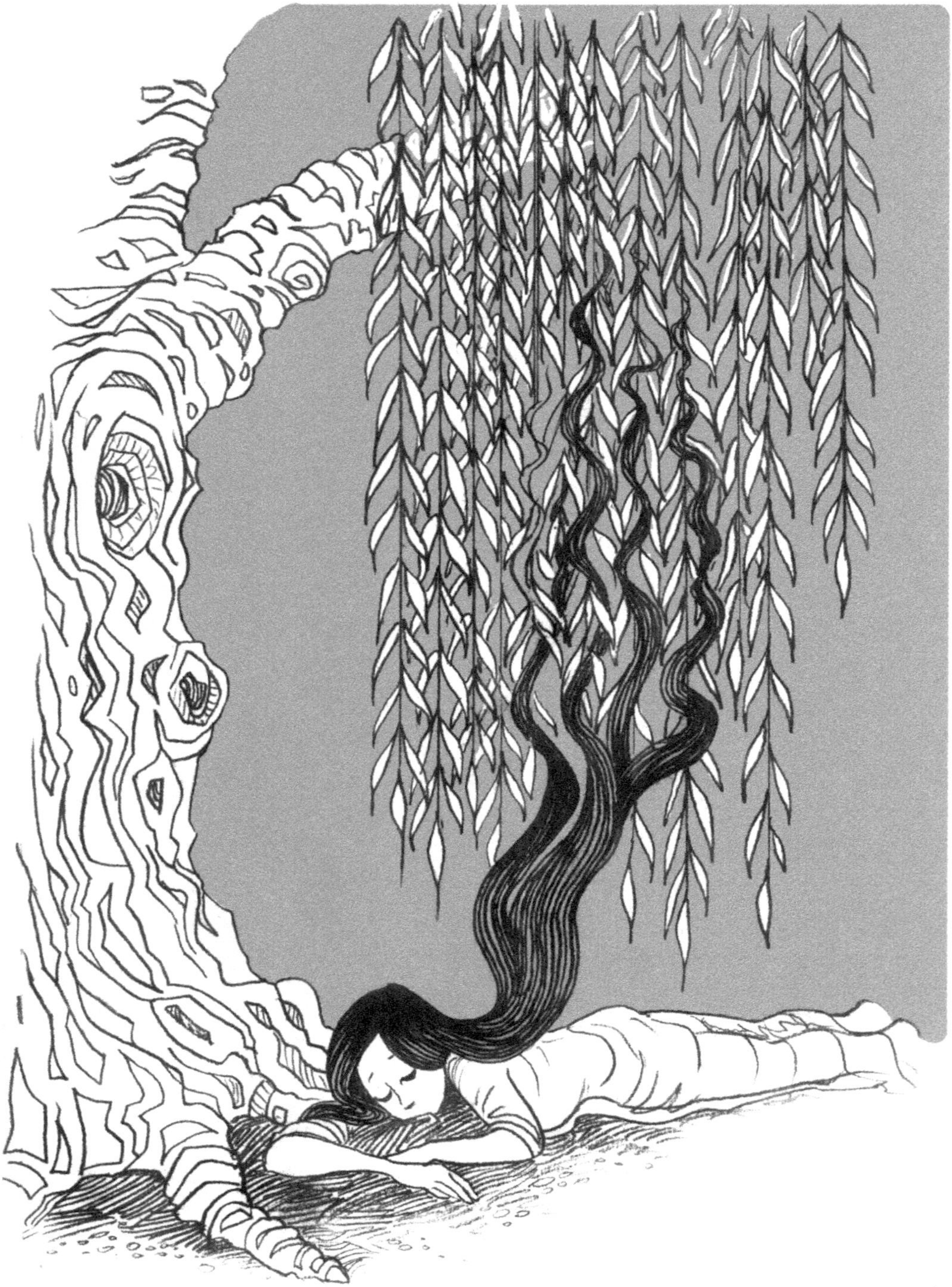

1. THE MAGIC REED

*I don't know if you believe in reincarnation, but I do because
I have been reincarnated as a Persian girl many times.*

I remember! Once in the tenth century, I occupied the body
of an-eleven-year-old girl named Noor, which means light.
I lived with my parents and three slightly older siblings—
two sisters and one brother, in Dyaar, a village at the extreme
north of Persia, near the border of Russia and close to the Caspian
Sea.

Every day Mom, Dad, and my brother Ali worked in the rice farm
from sunrise to sunset. My sisters spent their time with their neighborhood friends, or, if they were home, they kept together, ignoring me
completely. I was the only one taking care of the household tasks.

I looked forward to every evening. After dinner, I put my head on
my mother's lap for her to comb my long jet black locks. To me, it was
bliss but my sisters' constant complaints filled my ears. "Mama!" Batool, my oldest sister, grumbled, "Why do you spend so much time on
Noor's hair?"

"This is Noor's reward for doing the household chores. You two are
lazy and don't do anything."

Kobra, my second eldest sister turned a deaf ear. "If you brushed
our hair," she pointed to Batool's and her own coarse curly hair, "as
often as Noor's we'd also have the same."

"Nonsense! Allah has given her this beautiful hair," my mother
replied. "My brushing brings out its beauty."

One day, when Ali and my father had gone out before my mother
did, Batool rushed to her and said, "It's been a long time since we've
seen our aunt. Can we go for a visit?"

"It's a long walk to her house," my mother worried.

"It's only the next village," Batool pleaded, "If we leave now, we'll
get there before sunset."

"Are you taking Noor with you?"

Knowing they would not be allowed to go otherwise, Batool turned, looked at me and nodded.

"Dear! Three young girls going through the woods without any chaperone—not right!"

"No worries, Mama," I chimed in, happy that, for once, my sisters included me. "We'll keep each other company and protect one another."

"You girls won't be able to defend yourselves or each other." Her concern for us was obvious in her eyes and voice. "Wait at least until tomorrow so Ali can go with you. Who knows what you might encounter on your way—evil exists at every turn in the path."

"No, no!" Kobra jumped in. "We're old enough and don't need him."

Finally, our mother's resistance melted in the sun, as if it was butter, and she gave us permission to leave right away.

When the sun was in the middle of the sky, we arrived at a river. One direction or another, there had to be a bridge somewhere but we could not see it. We sighted a man sitting by the water. "Hey mister," Batool hollered. "how can we cross this creek?"

"For you, beautiful girls," *his flattering voice disgusted me,* "no worries! I'll be happy to carry you one by one to the other side."

'Such an outlandish solution!'

To my horror, one at a time, my two sisters hurried to climb on his back to get to the other side of the creek. They had no shame in touching a strange man as if they had forgotten they were Moslem girls and forbidden to do so! I, however, did not wait for my turn. I threw some stones into the shallow river, took off my shoes, and crossed the stream.

When I reached the other side, the flame of anger in my sisters' eyes did not escape me. They were whispering. They were worried I would tell our father the sin they committed. So they lagged behind. *Allah was my witness! I had no intention to tell on them.*

After a short walk, Batool called me, "Noor! Stop!" She came and put her arms around me, "You look tired dear! Let's sit and rest under this tree."

I looked. It was a very majestic old tree. Its branches were touching the ground. We sat down. Batool leaned against its trunk, and wanted me to put my head on her lap so she could caress my hair. I was happy for her kind gesture. Like a lamb, I followed. She and Kobra started singing a lullaby. With the nearby sea breeze on my cheeks and the chirping of nightingales, I believed I was in paradise. Soon I dozed off.

How long was I sleep? I had no idea.

All of a sudden, I was awakened by a growling lion. I opened my eyes. There was no sign of my sisters. I felt an excruciating pain in my head when I tried to get up. Right away, I realized the willow branches had entangled my tresses. The more I tried to go forward, the more the willow branches pulled me backward. There was no way for me to escape. Then, I beseeched the lion, "King of the jungle, I beg you. Have mercy on me!"

"No mercy for you today! Your sisters sent me to eat you instead of them for you're prettier." The lion licked his mouth, "And they're right."

I realized I had to face my fate. "Promise me…"

"What?" The irritable lion said.

"Eat me in a way that my blood doesn't fall on the ground—except for one drop."

"Okay! Whatever!"

When he pushed his fangs into my throat, he made sure that only a single drop of my blood trickled down onto the ground. Magically, a radiant stalk of reed grew instantly on its spot.

After a few days, my father came to look for me. When he reached the willow tree, he found my torn clothes. Knowing the area was a major habitat of lions, he understood the bitter reality. He wept and moaned. Right before leaving, he noticed a shining stalk of reed. He cut it, took it home, carved it, and made a lustrous flute out of it. When he started playing, instead of a melody he heard my voice:

Play, play, Daddy,
You play well Daddy,
Your lewd daughters tricked me,
Gave my hair to the willow tree,
And my body to the lion.

He fainted in shock. My mother, heeding the commotion, rushed into the room. She saw the flute, picked it up, and breathed into it.

Play, play, Mama!
You play well, Mama!
Your lewd daughters tricked me,
Gave my hair to the willow tree,
And my body to the lion.

After listening to me, my mother also passed out. My brother came, picked up the flute, blew in it and heard:

Play, play, my brother,
You play well, my brother,
Your lewd sisters tricked me,
Gave my hair to the willow tree,
And my body to the lion.

It seemed Batool heard my voice. Thinking I was back, she banged the door open, bolted in, snatched the flute from Ali, and threw it into our fireplace. The flute body crackled in the fire. As if by magic an ember floated out into the air and fell on a watermelon seed in the garden of the palace.

Back in my house, my brother was screaming and calling my sisters 'liars' for they had told them I was staying with my aunt. When my parents came to their senses, they too realized the harsh fact.

On the day of my funeral, all the villagers came to mourn my death, except my two sisters.

The following summer, because he was not able to find a suitable wife, the dashing crown prince took a walk in the garden. There he came across an enormous watermelon. Curiosity overtook him. He separated the watermelon from its vine with his dagger and tried to cut it when he heard,

"Oh! My hand!"
"Oh! My foot!"
"Oh! My head!"

He dropped the melon on the ground. It cracked open and I stood up. My knee-high locks covered my bare, womanly body. Right away, the prince enveloped me with his cape. Staring into my eyes, he said, "This is magic! You are beautiful! Who are you?"

"I am Noor!" I said. While I told him of my odyssey, I could read in his eyes admiration and love.

"Such a fascinating heroic life!" he said. "Allah has sent you to me. Would you be my bride?"

Unbelievable! Our handsome prince is asking me to marry him!

"Yes!" I replied graciously.

A guard was sent to fetch my family for the wedding. Shivering and cowering before me in fear, my two sisters knew well I could inflict any punishment on them—even death. Yet, I decided not to mention any-thing of their diabolical act. For me, it was all forgotten and ever since, I've owed my good fortune to my wicked sisters.

In later years, our king abdicated. His son, my husband, became the king. And *I*, the shining REED, came to be the queen.

Because of what my sisters did to me, I grew to be courageous and forgiving—fit to be the Queen of Persia!

I hope you agree with me! Sometimes the worst thing in life can turn out to be the best thing!

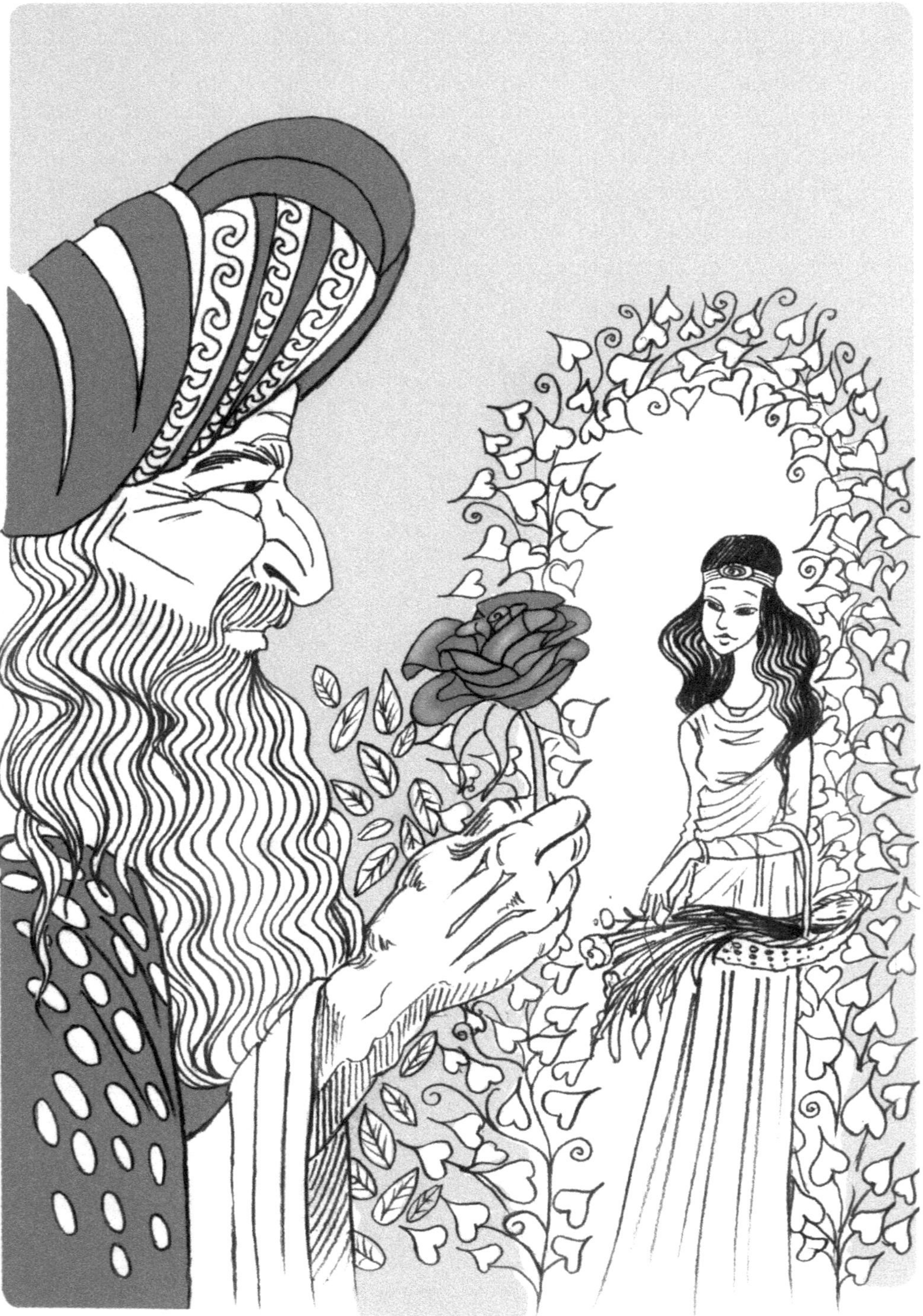

2. THE GARDENER & THE PRINCESS

*I don't know if you believe in reincarnation, but I do because
I have been reincarnated as a Persian girl many times.*

 remember! Once, I lived as a seventeen-year-old Persian Princess, Roxana, in the year five hundred before the birth of Christ. The capital of Persia, Persepolis, was the light of the world and my father, King Darius, was the ruler of the entire Persian Empire. We believed in one God, *Ahura Mazda,* the ultimate force of goodness and we were well aware of the Devil, *Ahriman.* We, women, were not wearing veils; it would take another twelve hundred years until we were forced to cover our heads.

One day during my stroll in the garden, I had a strange encounter with the head gardener. He was wearing a white garment—*'gardeners don't wear white!'* I was baffled. He offered me a white rose on that cold winter day and asked me to carry it at all times. "Promise me!"

"What?" I smiled.

"When you will have a problem that no one else can solve," he said in a soothing voice, "come to me, even if it's on your wedding night." As I gazed at him, I felt my heart filled with divine love. So reluctantly, I nodded. *'How was this possible? My father, the most powerful man, had all the wise men and scholars at his fingertips. No way would I need this old man.'*

Three months later, on the first day of spring, while we were celebrating our New Year, *Nowrooz,* I met and fell passionately in love with the prime minister's son, Afsheen, a handsome and sturdy young man. He and I met numerous times in secret. At last, I could keep our love hidden no more. I broke the news to my father and asked for his permission to marry Afsheen. He told me instead that according to a rumor, evil sometimes possessed Afsheen. Because my father had been sent by God to endorse righteousness among his people, he simply could not and would not allow me to marry a man who was seized by the Devil.

I, myself, had never witnessed this ailment. To oppose my father's wish, I went on a hunger strike and fell ill. My father could not bear to lose his only child. He gave me permission to marry Afsheen.

My wedding ceremony was certainly unfit for a princess. It was a hush, hush wedding. My father did not even attend it. However, I was excited that I would be Afsheen's lawful wife.

Right after the priest pronounced us 'husband and wife' we were sent to Afsheen's castle. That very night in the bridal chamber, I observed my beloved husband possessed by the evil force for the first time. He began shaking and fell down while foaming from his mouth. I had no idea what to do. I called for help but no one came.

In a fog of despair, I remembered the gardener. I took out the white rose which until then was hidden in my bosom and rushed toward the palace. The path was long and dark. I heard a whisper. "Princess Roxana!"

When I looked around, a wolf had blocked my way. *'How strange! Wolves don't talk.'* I said, "Look!" I showed the white rose to the wolf. "I'm on a mission. My husband is possessed by the evil force. I'm on my way to find the gardener in the white garment. Hopefully he'll help."

"Wow! Princess, you put yourself in danger to save your husband," said the wolf. "I'm famished; so I'll wait for your return. I'd love to taste royal flesh under my teeth!"

Not long after that I noticed a flame in the distance. I was close to a dragon. It was breathing fire and blocking my way. The dragon also wanted to eat me. But, after he saw the rose and I explained my mission, he let me go. While he breathed out a very large flame, he said, "I'll be here waiting for you."

When I was just about to get through the gate to my father's palace, a lion jumped in front of me. "Princess! What are you doing here? Even the bravest men do not come to the jungle at this time of the night."

"I am on a mission! I'm about to lose my husband to the Devil." I showed him the white rose. "I'm going to find the gardener in white."

"Go ahead!" the lion said. "Because you endanger yourself to save another life, I will let you pass." He stepped away from the gate. But, "I'll be here waiting for you."

In spite of the darkness falling, I saw the gardener in his white garment. As soon as he saw me, he stood up and said, "Princess, what are you doing here at this time of the night?"

I described how the evil force had possessed the love of my life, my husband. He gazed at me and I felt my soul at peace. He reached in his pocket and took out a small bag. "This is holy rose powder that can ward off evil from your husband. Divide it into three equal parts, and everyday give him one part with water. This potion must be handled by a woman unaccustomed to any sin."

"Will the Devil leave him for good then?" I asked.

"You are here on your wedding night as you promised," said the gardener. "I hope your wish comes true."

"On my way back, I have three other beasts waiting to eat me."

The gardener gave me a dried branch of a tree with an opening. He advised, "When they approach you, breathe into this and everything will be fine."

I thanked him profusely and ran out. On my way home, just as each brute—the Lion, the Dragon and the Wolf—was ready to tear me apart, I breathed into the stick. Suddenly, a heavenly melody filled the land. To my amazement each of the three animals calmed down at once and sat on the ground. "Princess," they said, "you've answered brutality with kindness. You were also more worried about your husband than your own life. You came back, even though you knew this is a dangerous path. Hurry back to him."

When I arrived at the castle, my husband was barely opening his eyes. I dissolved the first part of the powder in a glass of water and gave it to him.

After I gave him the magic powder for the second day, to my dismay, he became worse. He had attacks several times that day until he was on his deathbed.

I was beyond myself. After my long and dangerous journey, my beloved husband was not yet cured. I mulled over what the gardener had said, '*...this potion must be handled by a woman unaccustomed to any sin!*' After thinking throughout the night, I admitted, I had committed sin when I met Afsheen in secrecy and had been his lover. I had to wipe away my sins.

The next morning, I first performed the ritual cleansing by taking a bath and by putting on my white praying robe. Then, I walked through the garden and entered the temple where the holy fire was always lit in the fireplace. I stood before the fire, prayed and confessed my sins to God. At dusk, I felt the divine spirit enveloping me. During my prayer, I realized in the past, I had given in to the evil force by denying its existence. My father, King Darius, the shadow of God, had refused to accept my union with Afsheen. My husband and I had been diverted from the path of the Almighty.

When I finished my prayers, I set out for the royal palace. My ears were deaf to the guards shouting, "Princess, His Majesty is not available." I pushed him aside and rushed inside. In front of all the audience, I threw myself at the king's feet, kissed them and sobbed, "Father! I offended against God and you." I had trouble breathing. "Your Majesty…today I'm pleading for your mercy…give my marriage…your blessing."

King Darius was taken by my humility. He rose, took my arm, helped me up, and hugged me. "My dear Roxana, our Empire is based on following the Ultimate Goodness, Ahura Mazda." The King went on to say how important it was for everyone to walk with honesty and respect. After kissing my forehead, he said, " Your words of regret have touched our hearts." King Darious then issued a royal decree that blessed my marriage.

Afsheen was dying. I rushed to him. I gave him the third dose and told him the good news. And *behold!* The evil force was broken.

Upon the return of Afsheen's health, my father, King Darius, and all of Persia celebrated our wedding for seven days and nights. For the rest of our years, Afsheen and I were freed of the Devil. We lived happily under the protective Shadow of Ahura Mazda.

Ever since, I have been grateful to Him by sending the gardener as my guide and blessing me with an altruistic soul.

Whenever Afsheen and I looked out the window, we were in awe of a beautiful white rose bush in the garden. Miraculously, as the rose bush appeared in the garden, Afsheen's health had returned.

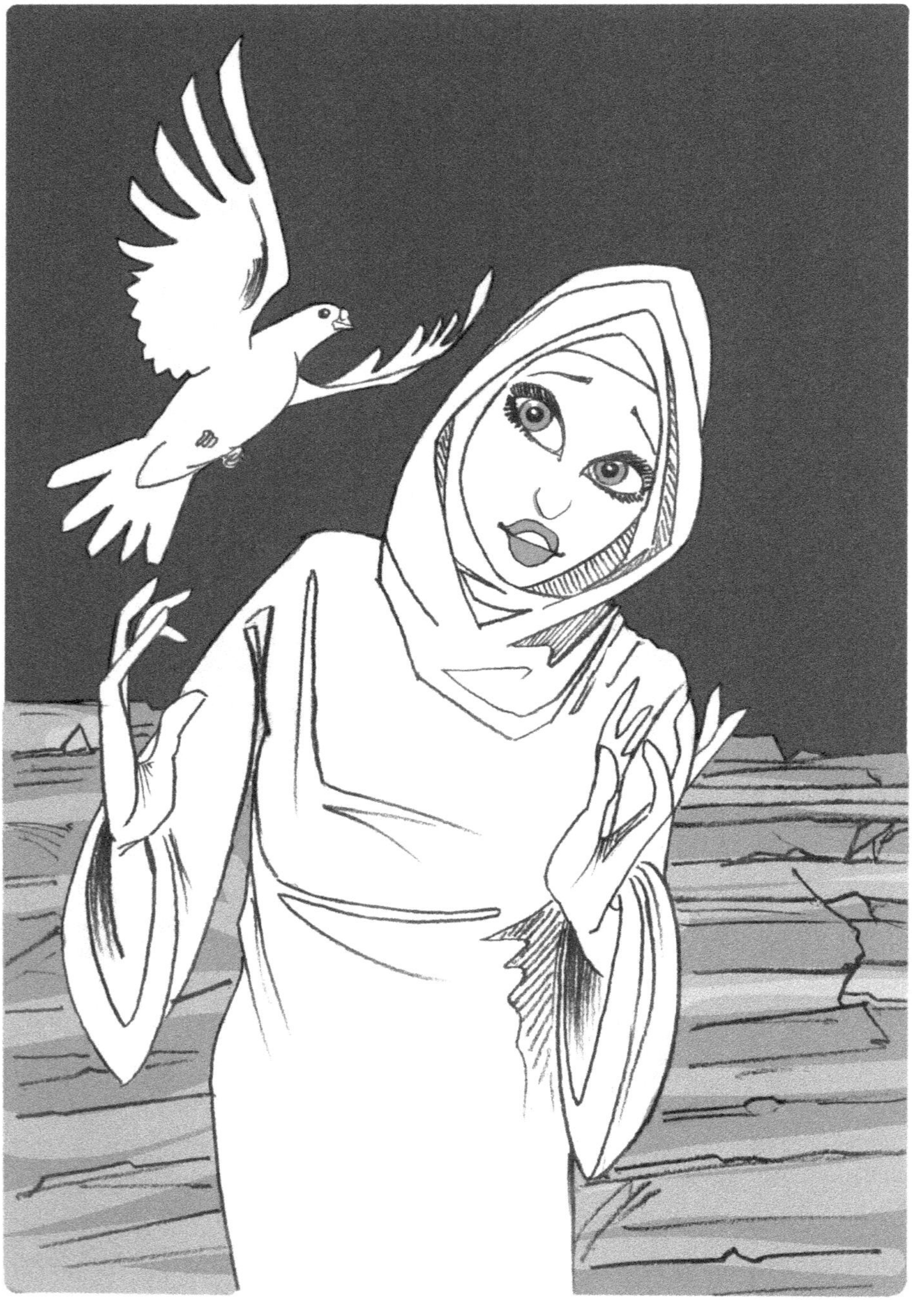

3. BRAVE ZARA

I don't know if you believe in reincarnation, but I do because
I have been reincarnated as a Persian girl many times.

I remember! It was eight hundred twenty-five years following the birth of Christ when I had life in the body of a ten-year-old girl, Golnaz. I lived with my family in the town of Kurd, in the southwest of Persia close to the Persian Gulf.

One day, while I was waiting outside for my friends, an old man in a green garment appeared before me. His kind voice drew me in. "Go to your mother and ask her if she remembers her promise to me."

I ran inside and asked, "Mama! What agreement do you have with the old man?"

Baffled, my mother, Zara, replied, "What old man?"

"The one in the green garment!" I responded.

"Come to me!" After she hugged me, she said with a heavy heart, "Let me tell you what's between me and the holy man. Get comfortable!" She began the story of her life journey taking me back to the time when she was a young girl.

It was almost thirty years ago. My mother had died giving birth to me. My father, Mirza, your grandfather named me, "Zara" and we lived in Baneh, a village by Mount Zagros in the northwest of Persia, close to Turkey.

My father, a shop keeper, was very proud of his Kurdish heritage. However, he was not very pleased with the majority of his tribe. They were the last group to put down their swords and accept Mohammad as their prophet. Unlike them, Mirza was a devoted Moslem and whole heartedly practiced Islam. In life, he had only one wish—to make the pilgrimage to Mecca in Saudi Arabia, so that he could have the title of haji in front of his name. Day in and day out, Mirza diligently put aside most of his earnings from his spice shop for the journey.

When I had reached the age of sixteen, one night my father said cheerfully, "Dear Zara, now I have enough money to go to Mecca."

I clapped, "Oh, *Baba*...I'm so happy."

At once, though, his face darkened like a cloudy sky, "My child! How can I leave you alone without a man to protect you?"

After some thinking, I responded to him with assurance that there was no reason to be worried. He needed to build a twelve-foot brick wall around the house, divert the nearby stream so water would come to the yard, and stock the storeroom with a year's worth of rice, salted leg of lambs and lards. I would then be safe and nothing could harm me.

"A year is long. Won't you be afraid to live by yourself for all that time?" Mirza asked.

I shook my head. Without a mother, I had long, since learned to fend for myself. I was never apprehensive for my safety. I had grown strong by climbing the mountain to bring fresh water home from its springs and by washing clothes in its streams close to my adobe house. I believed I could even race the neighborhood mountain panthers and win.

When the wall was finished according to my specifications, my father obtained the edible food items I had requested. In addition, he gave me self-defense lessons with his own sword and advised me to keep it under my pillow. Then, Mirza set out on his pilgrimage.

In the winter of that year, one night after a heavy snow, I was awakened by the sound of a click coming from the roof. At first, I thought it had to be an animal. Before falling asleep again, I heard two other clicks. The third one was much louder than the rest. I realized it had to be an intruder. I jumped out of bed, grabbed my father's sword from under my pillow, and looked through one of the windows. A lad was coming down from the ladder at the far side of the back yard. I cracked open the window and stood by it. When I saw him peeping inside, I wasted no time in swinging the sword down and cutting off his head.

Then I rushed to close the window. Shortly after that another young-ster began descending the ladder. I hurried to the second window, kept it ajar and hid behind the curtain. When he poked his head in, without any fear, I swiftly decapitated him too and closed the window.

"Mama Zara, you had to be brave and strong."

She wiped her sweat off her forehead, "Dear Golnaz, I remember, at that moment I ignored my loudly beating heart and hastened to the third window. My gut feeling was telling me there had to be an-other thief."

I made sure the third window was ajar and waited. At the mo-ment I brought down the sword, the third invader pulled his head back outside. He ran toward the ladder while holding his neck. Drops of his blood fell on the snow-covered ground.

My mother, Zara, touched her lips so no words came out. She closed her eyes as if she relived that horrible life experience again.

"Mama, how in the world could you kill those men?" I asked her.

"Dear Golnaz," she dried her tears, "I have no idea what came over me."

"Mama, your home was invaded, and you had to defend yourself all alone."

I spent the rest of the night cleaning the blood in my bedroom. With revulsion I tossed each decapitated head out the window. When I heard the roosters calling us to pray, I began preparing for my morn-ing prayers to sooth my soul. I went to the pond in the middle of the yard to perform the ritual ablution. Once inside, I covered my head and stood facing Mecca after spreading my prayer rug. I raised my hands toward the sky and asked Allah's forgiveness. At dawn, I rushed to the magistrate's office to report the home invasion. Some of the al-dermen walked back with me, put the bodies on stretchers and covered them. They noted the runaway intruder's blood in the snow.

One of them affirmed, "Young lady, you clearly acted in self-defense. Very likely they knew you were alone, so they came to have their way with you!"

"They knew Mirza had not much money," the other one murmured.

"You're a woman warrior. Getting rid of evil souls is a righteousness act!"

After I was exonerated of any wrong doing, I breathed a sigh of a relief. Then, I was certain the Almighty also forgave me.

The following year my father, Haji Mirza, returned home, and his friends came to congratulate him. After that, he kept talking about one of his friend's sons, Ahmad. "Zara, he's such a nice boy that I hope one day he will be my son-in-law." I kept quiet. From time to time, Ahmad came with expensive gifts to the house to visit my father. I was never allowed to meet him.

As you know, dear Golnaz, "Traditionally, a Moslem girl is not supposed to come before a young man unless her marriage to him was forbidden." My mother swallowed and continued.

That coming spring, when the weather became pleasant and the fruit trees were covered with blossoms, one day Ahmad came to our house. When he left, my father called me to him, "Dear Zara, I'm very excited today."

"Why?"

"Ahmad asks your hand in marriage. And he has my permission to marry you. He's an honorable man. He would take good care of you!"

I was disturbed and unable to verbalize my opinion. Commonly in Islam, a girl's father would choose a husband for her.

I had no other choice, but to heed my father, "Tomorrow he will come to take you with him to his village where he will marry you."

"Why can't we marry here?" I bravely questioned my father, Haji Mirza.

"Ahmad's father is seriously ill, so your matrimony will be in his village."

The next day, Ahmad came. After my father called me into the room, he put my hand in Ahmad's and said, "I give you permission to marry my daughter, Zara. When you get home, you shall wed her officially." Then both men shook hands. Haji handed Ahmad a sack containing silver dishes, two candlesticks and several gold coins as my *dowry* — a bride's gifts to her husband.

"Mother Zara, but my father's name is Kamal, not Ahmad!"
"Be patient my child!"

My journey with my husband to be was about a day's walk through the woods. I was bewildered. *'Ahmad was taking me along a rugged winding road instead of the usual route.'* But I was not supposed to question anything that my future husband did. Ahmad was silent for half of the way with me walking behind him. All of a sudden, he stopped, whirled around, dropped the sack on the ground and tore off his neck scarf. He pointed to the scar and screamed, "Do you know who gave this to me?"

I couldn't believe my eyes. I was absolutely terrified by having to confront this evil man again. He quickly retrieved a rope he had hidden in his garments, grabbed my hands and tied them, turning a deaf ear to my pleading, "Please let me go!"

No one else was there either, as if in this whole world, he and I were the only ones. He dragged me behind a clump of bushes and tied me to a tree.

"I wish I would've killed you that night," I fumed.

"Zara, I'm not done with you yet!" Ahmad growled, baring his teeth. He snatched my scarf from my head and shoved it in my mouth. "You're going to suffer greatly for what you did." He checked the knots in the rope one more time tying me to the tree and as he started walking away he shouted over his shoulder, "Once I come back with some firewood, I will burn you to death."

I tried to wiggle myself free but found it impossible. Some time after, the sound of a clickety-clack caught my attention. I saw that an old man in a green garment with his wagon approached me.

"Golnaz, we Moslems believe that whoever fights evil forces is protected by saints and angels sent by Allah. But the ones who have committed sins are unable to see their green garments."

"Mama Zara, I saw him in his green garment."

"Yes, my dear! You are a child and all children are innocent."

The man's voice calmed me as he removed the gag. "Who tied you up?"

"Saint Khizr! Please save me." I burst to tears and begged him, "My evil husband-to-be is coming back to burn me."

After untying me, Saint Khizr helped me onto his wagon. He piled up several pieces of wood around me; so that I couldn't be seen. He continued on his way. A few miles down the main road, he came upon a huge courtyard where some merchants had stayed overnight. The old man also decided to stop and rest at this caravansary.

Suddenly, Ahmad's voice shattered the air above me, "Hey! Old man, have you seen a pretty girl wandering around?"

"Allah may bless you! Here I am with my mule and lumber right before your eyes! Do you see any girl here?" the old man responded.

Ahmad yelled, "She has to be somewhere here although the head of the merchants hasn't seen her either!"

The old man scoffed, making a shooing motion. "Go! Go away!"

When it was safe, Saint Khizr removed the pieces of wood hiding me and took me to the head of the merchants. When the merchant laid eyes on me, he told the old man, "I'm Mehran Khan of the town of Kurd. Leave the girl with me. She will make a suitable wife for my son."

"Then, the old man left you with Mehran Khan, my grandfather!" My joyful voice filled the room.

"At the time," my mother, Zara, said, "I was still worried about my safety and future, but happy that I had been rescued from the wicked Ahmad. Mehran Khan kindly asked me my name and my hometown. I murmured, 'Zara, from Baneh'."

Standing before the Chief Merchant, I felt helpless. I had no strength to express my wish to be sent back home to my father, Haji Mirza. I couldn't believe I was the same girl who had cleaned the world of two heinous fellows. Instead, I felt like a worm without any spine. Or, maybe deep down, I thought, I dare not to return to Baneh where Ahmad might easily find me. Silently I prayed to Allah to protect me. Surely, Saint Khizr would not leave me with an evil man. I covered myself from head-to-toe with a cloak, climbed onto one of the camels in the middle of the caravan. It took several days until the convoy reached Kurd.

I was amazed at Mehran Khan's huge house with its exuberant garden. At the outskirts of the yard, there was a building with several rooms, *birooni,* quarters for men and on the left, *andarooni,* housing for women. Connected to these two buildings was a large community room which was a dinning room with a kitchen next to it. And there was no way to miss the two panthers chained to a post in the backyard.

Right away, I was sent to live with the women. On my way there, I heard Mehran Khan ordering the preparation for the wedding. Customarily in those days, the decision of the groom was not solicited either. Kamal had to obey his father's wish too. For the wedding, a messenger was sent to Baneh to inform my father that I was safe and ask his permission for me to marry Kamal.

After a month had passed, on the night before the wedding, Mehran Khan called me to his presence. When I entered, he said. "I sent a messenger to your father." He paused.

Something in his voice distressed me. I dared to raise my head to look into his eyes.

"Today, my messenger brought sad news to us."

I gasped, "What is it?"

"Your father, Haji Mirza, has passed on—Allah bless his soul."

I fell to the floor as if my legs could bare my body no more.

"I am so sorry!" Mehran Khan helped me stand up. "From now on, I will be your protector as well as Kamal's."

I had no time to mourn as the wedding took place in spite of my loss. By law, I could not live in the house without being married to Kamal—a young Moslem girl residing under the roof of a stranger was proscribed. The following day I wiped my tears as I put on my white dress, covered my head with a white scarf and announced my acceptance of marriage to Kamal in the presence of the Moslem priest, even if in my heart, I was crying for my father, Haji Mirza.

On the wedding night, after all the guests had left, Kamal and I were sent to the bridal chamber. In the middle of the night, I had a horrible nightmare. Ahmad had found me and was determined to kill me. Without being aware of it, I bolted out of the room crying and pulling my hair. In the morning, an angry Kamal went to his father complaining about his bride.

They called for me and Mehran Khan asked, "What's wrong Zara? Have you lost your mind?"

"No!" I boldly retorted him, "But, at night I'm frightened. Please enclose the house with a twelve-foot brick wall, and leave the panthers unchained in the backyard to roam. Then I will sleep comfortably."

Mehran Khan did what I asked of him.

A year or so later, one night when Kamal had gone out of town, I opened my eyes in horror to find Ahmad cupping his hand over my mouth with a knife to my throat. In a low voice so as not to awaken the rest of the household, he threatened, "If you scream, I'll kill you. Listen to me carefully."

My heart thumping, I stood up and obeyed him. But instead of going to the side window where he had entered, I led him to the open one facing the backyard. Meanwhile, I began to pray under my lips, "Oh, Saint Khizr! I'm calling on you! I dedicate my first child—girl or boy—to you. Help me get rid of this evil man for good!"

I had no idea what happened, yet, in the blink of an eye, as if I received from the Almighty the same strength as when I got rid of Ahmad's two other devilish friends, I gained the upper hand and freed myself from his grip. Standing at the edge of the window, Ahmad lost his balance and tumbled down to the courtyard below.

I watched Ahmad slowly getting to his feet, making a quick-check of his extremities—no broken bones. As he turned to make a hasty retreat, he found in front of him the two black panthers—poised to spring upon him. In the next instant, the beasts sailed through the air. As they landed against his chest, they sank their fangs into his neck. The panthers' massive and powerful jaws soon dismantled Ahmad limb by limb.

In the morning, Mehran Khan called me to the backyard where Ahmad's remaining pieces were scattered all over. He said, "See, for your sake, a man got killed. This poor thief didn't deserve to lose his life over it."

"Trust me Mehran Khan," I said, looking him square in the eyes, "he was no poor thief. From now on, if you choose, you don't have to let these panthers free. I'm not afraid of anyone or anything anymore."

"The following year, Allah completed our happiness by giving you, my dear Golnaz, to us." Mother Zara hugged and kissed me.

"Wow! Mama! Such a fearless life you had!"

"Dear! Next time when Saint Khizr appears to you, tell him, 'My daughter is yours, as I vowed.'"

It took seven years before I saw the Saint again. When I repeated my mother's words, he said without blinking, "Listen to me carefully. Because of your mother's bravery in getting rid of the three evil spirits, from now on, you are safeguarded by Allah—The Good Spirit. Your fate is also the same as your mother's—fighting evil souls." He paused. "Whenever you laugh, roses will appear around you. At any time you cry, it will rain. A sack of gold will appear at the entrance door when you enter someone else's house. Lastly, your soul is a pearl, placed in the heart of a deer with no horns and a white spot on its forehead."

With these words, Saint Khizr vanished. I ran inside and explained everything to Mother Zara. *Happily* she kissed me. I laughed and *Behold!* Many roses emerged around me.

When I was eighteen years old, one day the Prince of Arabia, Satar, saw me from a distance while he was on one of his hunting trips. On that day, my veil had fallen away as I rode a camel with my friends. From that moment, he sought to ask my hand in marriage. My parents were delighted. They prepared my dowry and made me ready for my journey to my husband's country.

My father had a sister, Tamra. Throughout the years, I heard gossip about my aunt being a witch. Just before my wedding, I even heard she and her husband got into a big fight and *poof* he was not around anymore. But I never believed any of it. Tamra, my aunt was always very kind to me. A few days before my journey to my husband's homeland, Tamra pleaded with me to take her and her daughter, Tara, to my new homeland since I would not have the company of any other family members. I agreed.

On the day of my journey, I wore my veil, hijab, and wept for leaving my parents. I mounted a horse and departed for my new homeland. Meanwhile, Tamra and Tara rode their camels at the back of the entourage far from the rest.

At sunset on the first day, we camped in some woods. The men were in separate tents from the women. In the middle of the night, I was awakened by Tamra's shaking, "Golnaz, wake up dear! Our campfire is out, let us get some firewood."

As I rubbed my eyes and covered my head, I followed Tamra out into the dark. When we were far away from the tents, she suddenly attacked me. I was so bewildered that I could do nothing. Tamra snatched my scarf and tied my hands with it. Then she ripped part of my skirt and fastened my feet to a tree. She flung evil black dust in my eyes. They turned into marbles! She took them out, put them in my pocket and sneered, "Now, let's see if *your* holy man can rescue you!" She cackled as she set off back to the camp. All of my crying and wailing fell on deaf ears under the now pouring rain.

I felt the warm morning sun on my skin as I heard footsteps. I cried out, "Whoever you are, please untie me and take me home with you."

"What happened to you?" a man asked.

"Please! Please!" I begged.

"As Allah is my witness!" He responded in a sad voice. "I'm a poor wood cutter and can barely feed my three daughters."

"I won't be a burden on you and your family. I promise."

After a long pause, he replied, "Let me go and ask them. I will come back to take you only if they agree."

While I was waiting and thinking how I could free myself, I heard him again, "My youngest daughter, Mina, does not mind to share her food with you." He kindly untied me and took me to his home. "I'm Mina!" She took my hand, "As my friend—sister, from now on I divide whatever I have with you."

I was touched by her generosity. I whispered to her, "Take me out for a while!"

Mina took me for a short walk. When we came back, she announced, "I wonder how this sack appeared by our door." Then I heard her joyful voice, "Allah! I can't believe my eyes! A sackful of gold coins!"

Every day, I left the house two or three times and, miraculously, each time there was another sack of gold at the door. "Dear Golnaz! You've brought good fortune to us. Now, we're rich and our father is not a wood cutter anymore."

Several years passed. One day as Mina was taking me to a neighborhood wedding celebration, there was a sudden flash of light. In an instant, I found myself inside a cave. I could hear Mina outside wailing, "Golnaz! Where are you? I can only see a huge cave with no opening! I'm scared!" I could hear her crying… soon there was silence.

But after a short while, Mina returned with her father who tried to move the smooth rounded boulder which was blocking the entrance to the cave. It wouldn't budge. He called on his workers. With their pickaxes and chisels, they attacked the rock. I hoped that with so many men, they would be able to rescue me. After what seemed a very long time, they had only succeeded in making a small hole in the huge boulder. And when they took a break, *'Behold!'* the rock returned to its original shape in the blink of an eye. They tried and tried, but to no avail. At last, tired and defeated, they went home. When the outside sounds stopped, I circled the inside of the cave by touching the walls. Suddenly, I heard the chirping of nightingales and the delicious smell of flowers. Then and there, I understood that the cave had appeared to protect me from my aunt's witchcraft. I remembered Saint Khizr's words, *'The Good Spirit protects you.'*

I prayed to Allah for my freedom as I fell into a deep refreshing sleep. I dreamt:

After Tamra left me in the woods, she crept into my husband, Satar's tent, spread black magic dust on him and chanted, 'By the power of Satan, whenever you look at Tara, you will see Golnaz instead.' She then dressed Tara, my look alike cousin, in my clothes. Tara mounted my horse and they all went to the land of Arabia. So, Tamra tricked my husband into believing that Tara was me. Yet, he could not understand his wife's cruel behavior toward everyone, especially to him. And so, he stayed away from home most of the time.

Tamra discovered that I was still alive by throwing dried bones on the ground. She went to 'Prince Satar, and said, "Your wife is very ill. To cure her, you must track down a deer with no horns and a white spot on its forehead." One day, Satar hunted a deer with no horns and a white spot on its forehead and took it to his palace. Right away Tamra gutted the animal. When she took out its heart, a pearl dropped to the floor and rolled away into a corner. Tara devoured its heart but of course, no cure came to her. Meanwhile Satar continued his wandering far away from Tamra and Tara.

Meanwhile in the cave, I knew not how long I had slept when to my surprise I heard a man's voice. "Who are you?"

"I am Golnaz!" I was startled into replying for I knew so far no-one had been able to come inside the cave.

"Who did you say you are?"

"Golnaz!"

"How can that be? She's my wife and is in Arabia." The man said in disbelief.

"Are you Prince Satar then, my husband?"

"It would seem so."

"My wicked aunt, Tamra, used Black Magic to blind me. But here, in this cave, Saint Khizr protects me."

"Then you must be the girl I fell in love with in Persia"

He hugged and kissed me, and said, "You are indeed my wife. Let us get out of this cave at once."

I shook my head. "If Tamra sees us, she will use her evil magic to kill both of us."

"I know Allah wants us to be together. I was able to move the rock at the cave door as soon as I touched it—Allah's will!"

"Tamra's spell is of extreme force…first, we must find a way to defeat her once and for all. Now go home my beloved husband and be careful not to raise any suspicions."

Unwillingly, Satar left the cave.

From then on, using the ruse of a hunting trip, Satar continued to visit me. After nine months Allah blessed us with a son. We named him Safa.

When our son was one year old, Satar took him to the palace. My heart wept as Satar left with my little boy, but I knew it was for Safa's own good to be raised in his father's palace instead of in a cave.

Satar presented him as an orphan and demanded that Tara and Tamra take good care of him. "If he loses even one wisp of hair, I will banish both of you from the palace!"

During their absence, I thought about how my mother Zara had instructed me to beseech Allah and Saint Khizr to help me to get rid of the evil forces. Day in and day out, I prayed, until one day a bird flew to me. I felt the bird carefully taking my eyes from my pocket with its smooth beak. One by one, this bird put my eyes back into their sockets and patted them with its feather. *Behold!* As I opened my eyes I could see a white dove was before me. Then, she disappeared.

One day not long after, Satar entered the cave. He saw my eyes were open and I was looking directly at him. He took a bright pearl from his pocket. In a joyful voice he said, "Golnaz look! This morning our son found this."

The pearl's beauty mesmerized me. I caught it, raised it to my lips to kiss it when it rolled from my hand into my mouth and I swallowed it. As I did so, the cave disappeared! The wood-cutter and his daughters who came by weekly to pray were there. And all cheered when they witnessed my appearance at the very spot.

Prince Satar took me to his palace and proclaimed, "This is my lawful wife, Golnaz."

My evil aunt, Tamra, conjured up all of the Black Magic she knew but to no avail. I was protected by the Good Spirit of the pearl.

I could have had my aunt and cousin beheaded if I wished but I decided against it. And yet their evil could not go wholly unpunished. So Prince Satar banished them to a far away pig farm where they would spend the rest of their days.

My husband and I went on to live a happy life. Generation after generation, we were blessed and protected by "the Good Spirit". And all of this was possible because my mother, brave Zara, confronted the evil forces and cleansed the world of three diabolical spirits.

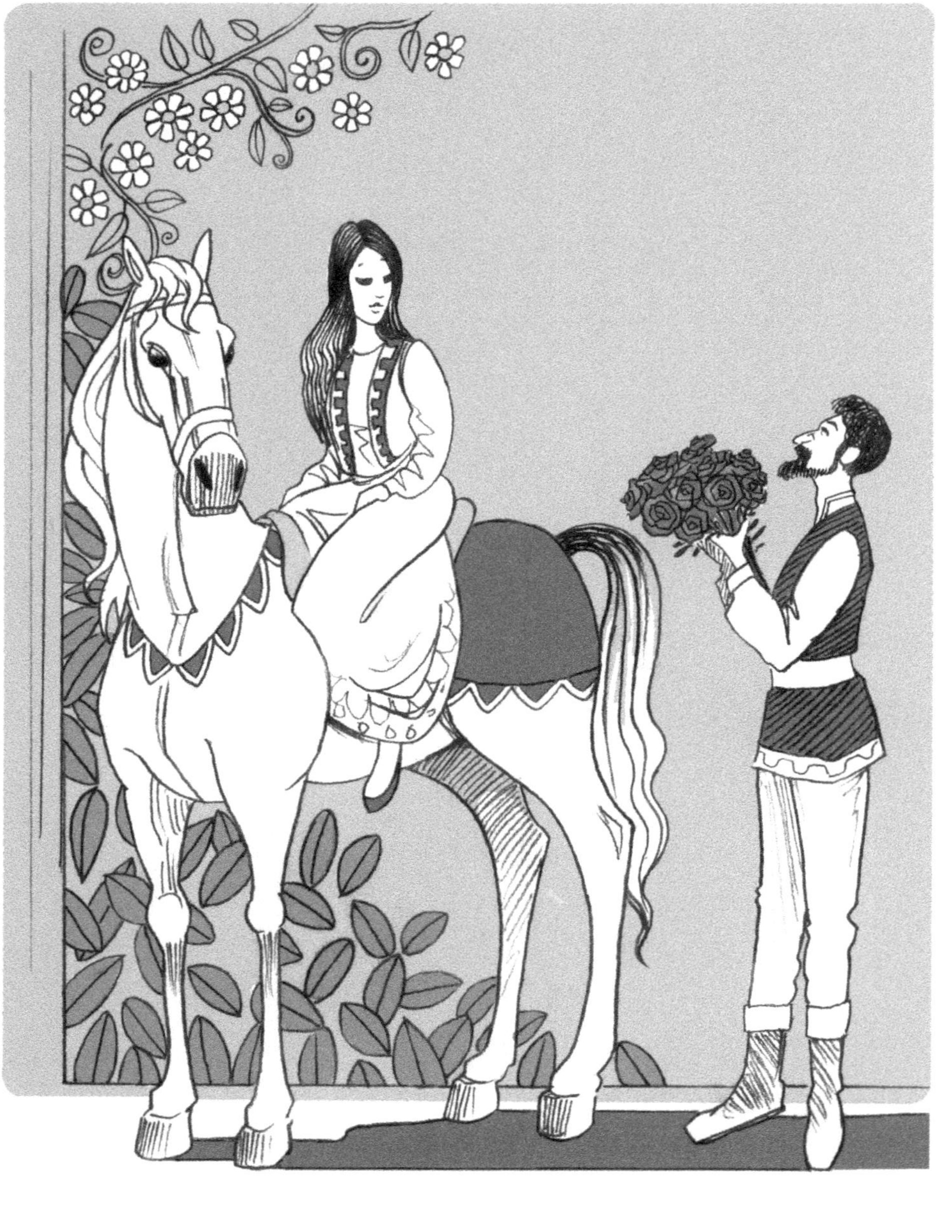

4. THE TAILOR'S DAUGHTER AND THE CHIEF MERCHANT'S SON

I don't know if you believe in reincarnation, but I do because I have been reincarnated as a Persian girl many times.

I remember! Once I was a fifteen-year-old girl named Sahar in the mid-nineteen-twenties living with my parents and two older sisters in Tehran, the capital of Persia.

My father was a renowned tailor with many rich clients who constantly traveled between Tehran and Paris. Every night we waited anxiously for his return to tell us the news of the "fairyland"— Paris. His report was usually the same. "Paris is breaking with all traditions, especially in fashion. This century is headed for an uproar!"

"How come?" I asked.

"Over there, women now dare to wear something called 'flappers'!"

"What is that?" My mother inquired.

"Short skirts—just come to their knees!" Baba shouted, "Blaspheme!"

"Dear Baba…"

"Yes, Sahar?"

As I looked into his angry eyes, I swallowed my words, *'Why are we still covering ourselves up with veils?'* I loved to hear that women in the West dared to break with tradition and fashion.

My heart's wish, however, was to get married and be a mother. But my two other sisters were not married, and so it was impossible for my father to agree to my matrimony until they were. I prayed and put my trust in God to bring me a husband.

One night, my father came home, rushed to his room and slammed the door shut behind him.

We were all baffled. A few minutes later, my oldest sister, Sima, went to his room. She came out with wrinkled brows, shrugging her shoulders as she went to our mother. Then, Saba banged open the door to his room and went inside. She remained in there even less than Sima. When Saba bolted out, she said, "I don't have time to solve his ridiculous problem!"

Taking a deep breath, I brewed a pot of fresh tea. I went to his room. After greeting him, I put the tea tray down in front of him and sat down quietly beside him. "Dear Baba have some tea!"

"My child, Sahar, a heavy load is on my shoulders! I don't think all of the tea in the world will help."

"What's bothering you, Baba?"

"Today, a special client—the Chief Merchant's son, Amir, stopped by."

"Wow! He must have heard of your fame and talent!"

He nodded, "Amir's request was very peculiar!" Baba put a sugar cube in his mouth and sipped his tea.

"Did he want you to make him a garment out of silk?"

"I wish it was that simple," in a worried voice, he said. "He requested that I sew him a garment out of FLOWERS! Unbelievable!"

I smiled and said, "Father, Amir's given you a riddle!"

"A riddle?"

"Yes, he wants you to know his heart is empty of romance and he's asking if you have a daughter suitable for him to marry."

My father was quiet as I fell into my own thoughts. Soon though, my heart was filled with joy as I told my father, "Tomorrow ask the merchant's son for a thimble, a pair of scissors and a needle made out of flowers. Tell him that when you will have these items, you will be more than happy to make him the garment out of flowers!"

"What do these things mean?" My father inquired.

"The thimble is the symbol of my eldest sister who is not a deep thinker; the pair of scissors are for my second sister who is impatient and has a habit of cutting off everyone when they speak." I swallowed. "The needle represents *me* as I have a sharp mind. This way, Amir will know that I am the one who not only solved his riddle but I am giving him one in return." I couldn't help but laugh.

My father suddenly put his tea cup down. "My child, I'm afraid he will discredit me for requesting such silly things"

"Trust me, Baba!"

"How did you become so smart to be able to decipher the rich man's puzzle?"

"Every day, when the Dervish, storyteller, comes to our neighborhood, I go and listen to him…"

My father finished my thoughts, "Yes, I see, in the epic stories, sometimes the hero solves the king's riddle so that he may marry the princess!"

I smiled.

The following night, when my father returned home, he called me to his room. In a kind voice, he said, "Dear Sahar, you must be really gifted. As soon as I mentioned those three items to Amir, he became very happy and left the shop."

I was thrilled to pieces. My heart became filled with love for Amir. I thought, "He is smart and interesting because he does not wait to have a wife by way of an arranged marriage." I was confident that before long he would send his relatives to ask my father for my hand in marriage.

A week later we received the wonderful news. Amir's family would come to my house to talk with my family about the wedding arrangements.

A few days prior, my mother and our maid, Khadijeh, cleaned our guest room from top to bottom. They rolled our wall to wall ruby color rug outside the house and beat the dust out of it with sticks. Then, they washed the royal blue cushion covers and laundered the yellow silk bolster covers so that our guests would be soothed in the greatest comfort and style. Khadijeh polished our silver tea set. Varnishing our several copper or silver plates etched with the name of Mohammad, our prophet, or our saints, Ali, Hasan and Hossain, was another task of hers. We hung these memorabilia on the wall instead of picture frames because we used no pictures since in Islam, it is forbidden to draw or paint pictures of people. We believed, "Allah is the only creator." As the last task, Khadijeh swept the portico and the huge backyard leading to the guest room.

I had no duties on the arranged day. My mother did not want me to look tired for our guests. Still, I was nervous and praying to God that the women, especially Amir's mother, would like me and not order me to open my mouth for them to see my teeth. I hated when someone treated me as if I were a cow or a horse—a demeaning request. God willing, everything would go smoothly and soon I would be Amir's wife.

On that day, I did my best to get rid of my negative thoughts. I took joy in washing, in combing my long hair and in wishing that my sisters would get married before me. My marriage to Amir would very likely be blocked—because of them not being married. As was tradition, our neighborhood matchmaker was well-aware of my sisters age—Sima seventeen and Saba sixteen—and way overripe to be wed. Usually, a girl was allowed to marry at age nine.

At last, Amir's mother and relatives arrived. After my mother greeted them, she led them to our guest room where my other aunts were. Khadijeh gave me one of our trays with six dainty tea cups filled to the brim with fresh tea to take in to our guests. On my way, I prayed for my heart to stop beating so loudly.

As I walked into the room, right away I noticed the lady who was sitting at the top of the room, in the seat saved for our most respected guest. She had to be Amir's mother, Lady Mehri. I met her kind eyes and felt as if an angel was touching my head, calming me. After I served her and everyone else, I dashed out. Staying behind the closed door, I waited to be called back in.

"My son, Amir, only desires your youngest daughter, Sahar!"

"How so, my lady?" I heard my mother's polite voice.

"Amir gave a riddle to your husband, and Sahar was the only one who could solve it." She paused. "In reality, Amir has been engaged to his paternal cousin, Goli, since they were born."

It was not odd. In those days, families of higher rank repudiated an alliance with poorer families. So, they engaged their cousins to each other even at their births. The boy and girl grew up with the under-standing that they had to marry each other. *'Bravo Amir! He's brave enough to break with the tradition...'* My mother's voice interrupted my thoughts. "Then, why doesn't he want to marry his cousin?"

"He knows he can never love Goli as his wife. He fancies to marry an intelligent girl. Sahar not only solved his riddle but returned it with one of her own. Amir has been insisting on getting permission from his father, Akbar Khan, the Chief Merchant, to marry your daughter."

Behind the door, I took a deep breath knowing that here would be no problem with my matrimony to Amir going forward. So, I went to my room.

A week later, when Amir's father, Akbar Khan, and his male relatives came to talk with my father and my side of the male family, I was like a dove soaring into the blue sky. In that meeting, they would negotiate and agree on an amount of money or gold which the groom would promise to my family. He would sign a promissory note, *mehrieh,* on the day of the wedding. In case of divorce or death, he or his survivors would pay to his wife such an amount. In return, my father informed Amir's family of the total amount of my *dowry,* household goods which I would take to my husband's house. Sad to say, it was more of a transaction than the unification of a man and woman. However, our Prophet Mohammad, Allah bless his soul, wanted to make sure we women had some way of supporting ourselves if something happened and our marriage ended.

After several visits from Amir's family to mine, all the details were ironed out and Akbar Khan set a date for my wedding. We heard that he had given his brother, Goli's father, a large parcel of land that was supposed to be her mehrieh. It seems he was remorseful not keeping his word to Goli's father.

Thanks be to Allah! Everyone was amiable and the announcement was made that Amir and I were engaged. As was customary, I expected to receive some gifts every now and then from Amir.

One day, a servant brought a huge tray and put it in front of me. A delicious smell filled the entire room. But as I uncovered the tray, I was flabbergasted. It was all a mess! The rice dish was supposed to be filled with neat heaps of fluffy rice covered with saffron. Instead, it was scattered in the eggplant stew. The whole roasted chicken was missing a leg and part of its breast. When I picked up the jug of juice, it was half full. *'What's this? Has Amir sent me a riddle or insulted me by sending his discarded food?'* So, without touching anything, I returned it with a message, "Why did you send me your leftovers?"

Several days passed and I heard nothing.

On the seventh day, a maid brought me a box. When I opened it, I found a pair of dirty white shoes. I was infuriated. They were supposed to be a pair of brand new white shoes for my wedding. I threw them back into the box and intended to return it with a message to call off my engagement. While I was taking a deep breath, I heard a jingle. My ears sharpened. It was the unmistakable sound of gold coins coming from the maid's pocket.

"Where did you get your gold coins?"

"I had them from a long time ago, my Lady!"

"If you are honest and tell me who gave them to you, I will even double them."

"My Lady! Forgive me! The Master Amir's cousin, Lady Goli, gave them to me !" She mumbled with a horrified face.

"Why?"

"She ordered me to wear these brand-new shoes in the mud." She paused and took out two gold coins out of her pocket. "See, my Lady! She gave me these as my tip."

I realized then that Goli had intercepted the servant with the food tray as well. I decided not to panic or do anything rash. After discarding the shoes in the trash, I breathed no word to anyone. I realized that Goli had to be jealous to her core. My wish was to marry Amir and I would do anything to stop her from meddling into my life.

It had become clear. Goli was determined to make me look unworthy in Amir's eyes. I began hearing untruthful rumors about me such as "I'm no good…have no social class…don't deserve to be Amir's wife."

Everyday there was new gossip around town. Like a spider, Goli was weaving her web in which she would ensnare Amir and me. At one point, I even learned Goli had gone to Amir's sister, Jamileh and her husband, Hossain, to plant seeds of malice in their hearts by saying that I might even not be a *virgin!* I tried to turn a deaf ear to all of the rumors. Yet every knock at our door made me panic that Amir was calling off our wedding.

One day, while I was helping my mother make my wedding quilt, I learned Goli was not the only one in opposition to this marriage. She informed me that my own father was still in doubt of giving his permission on the day of ceremony. I felt as if my heart was in my throat, choking me.

"Don't forget dear Sahar," My mother put down her scissors. "your father and I still have two unmarried daughters at home. How can you expect him to ignore our customs?"

I continued stitching while trying to calm the storm within me.

"Let me tell you a secret. Your father and I are very pleased that the Chief Merchant's only son is eager to marry you. But, how can your father go against a tradition that has been in existence for centuries?"

I begged my mother, "To Baba, your words are like water on a flame. I'm sure you can change his mind."

My mother smiled, "Let me see what I can do. Allah willing, everything will go smoothly."

'Believe it or not!' On the day of the wedding, all did go well and I thanked Allah for my good fortune—even Goli could do nothing to spoil it. To my surprise, Baba granted me his permission. He had broken with our tradition and allowed me to marry before my two older sisters. I was proud of him. So I said, "Yes" to the Mullah and accepted Amir as my husband. According to custom, without seeing each other, he and I became husband and wife. I breathed a little easier and anxiously waited for him to come to me. However, when Amir did come in, he did not unveil me or even say a word, before he dashed back out. My heart skipped a beat. Amir was my husband now and custom meant he should have unveiled me that night in the bridal chamber.

Later that night, Amir returned but he still did not uncover my face or even utter a word. He crossed to the other side of the room, and called out to the women waiting outside the closed door, "Don't expect to see any bloody handkerchief tonight or any night. Go away." He slept on a blanket and ignored my virgin quilt. As I cried quietly to myself I wondered how I could instill love in Amir's heart. I was no fool! I understood that this was Goli's work. She had created this distance between me and Amir. I could see that Amir believed all of the allegations against me.

Goli had succeeded in blackening me in Amir's eyes.

The next morning, before sunrise, I rushed to my mother-in-law, Mehri's room. Seeing me so distraught, she said, "I would like you to know that I never had any desire for Goli to be my daughter-in-law."

In awe I said, "But, she's your family member and I'm only a tailor's daughter."

"Yes, my child! But a tailor's daughter with an innocent heart is worth so much more than Goli with her dark heart." Mehri, like any other Moslem, counted her rosary and murmured, "I'm ashamed. Goli has filled the ears of Jamileh and her husband with lies about you which they have spread."

"I've heard!"

Mehri continued, "My dear, even Akbar Khan overheard Hossain whispering to some of Amir's friends that…"

I could no longer prevent my tears.

"Dear Sahar, not to cry! I believe in you. But being silent and doing nothing will not save your marriage."

"Will you help me?" I beseeched her.

Mehri nodded. "You are a smart girl. Let's wait a few days. So that Goli believes she has won."

Night after night, I slept in a separate room far from Amir, trying to think of a way to win over my husband. To my disappointment, he never asked for me.

After a few days, I felt as brave as a hero and ready to fight Goli, the monster blocking my bliss. I rushed going into Mehri's room and asked, "Where did Amir go this morning?"

"I think he's in the Yellow Garden."

"Is it possible to drape a horse all in yellow?"

"Surely! But why?"

"Dear Mehri," I looked directly into her eyes, "yellow is the color of happiness. Amir is looking for elation in the Yellow Garden."

With astonishment, she said, "My son is disappointed with his marriage to you! I understand!"

I put on yellow clothing, without wearing my veil. I used instead some make-up to enhance my beauty. I was quite apprehensive about not wearing my veil in public. *'No man ever hides behind a veil. Why should I?'*

I mounted the horse which was draped in yellow. I rode along a short path to the vast yellow garden. As far as my eyes could see, the landscape was covered with yellow daffodils.

"Hello?" I called out. As Amir came to the gate, I felt my heart thumping faster. I believed I may have even blushed. "May I have some of these beautiful daffodils?"

"Of course!" Amir replied while staring at me. Right away, he summoned one of his gardeners to bring a bouquet for me. "What is your name?" he asked.

I only gazed down at him and said nothing. As soon as Amir handed me the flowers, I galloped away.

I learned the next day that Amir was in the White garden. I changed my garments to all white, no veil, and mounted this time on a white horse. Before I left, Mehri asked, "Why white today?"

"Amir is in the White Garden looking for purity and innocence."

"He thinks his wife is stained!" Mehri exclaimed.

"Sadly so!" I sighed.

On my way to the White Garden, my heart was full of hope that I would show Amir I was as pure as the snow on the mountains.

"Today, will you tell me your name?" Amir asked the moment he saw me.

Like the day before, my lips were sealed. Mesmerized by the beautiful white carnations, I dared to gaze into his eyes, hoping to connect with his soul. I dashed away again as soon as he gave me the bouquet.

The third day, bubbling with excitement, Mehri said, "Today, Amir is in the Red Garden and a horse draped in red is waiting for you."

"Mama, you know what red means."

Mehri lit up, "Love dear! He's seeking love in his life."

"Red also signifies creation of life with its passionate energy." I smiled slyly. In my red wardrobe, I galloped my horse dressed in red toward the Rose Garden.

This time Amir was standing by the gate with an armful of roses. He brought the bouquet close to me and asked for my name. I refused to answer him. I grabbed the flowers with such force that their thorns wounded my hand, and my drops of blood spattered on him. "Alas my hand," I murmured and rushed out.

That night, I put on my veil and took Amir's dinner to him. When I put the tray down, he asked, "What happened to your hand?" I started to open the bandage and said, "Alas my hand!"

With eagle eyes, he stared at me in disbelief. He reached for my veil and removed it gently. "You are beautiful!" He kissed my hand and confessed he loved me from the moment he laid eyes on me in the Yellow Garden.

I said nothing as a smile of triumph covered my face.

"Now, I see how clever you are!"

"I was determined to show you." I paused. "I'm a fearless woman who will do anything to save her marriage."

"Even going out without a veil!" He lowered his head. "I was a fool. I believed Goli. Thanks to Allah, you saved our marriage."

"Goli was jealous."

"We must punish the Witch," Amir declared, "we should tie her by her hair to a horse and set it loose in the desert!"

"No! No!" I shook my head. "By killing one hateful person, we will create more hatred in others, such as in her parents."

"And if we get rid of them," he said, following my logic, "their relatives will come to take revenge."

"We will have to fight or live with a hateful throng. We can't possibly kill all of them!"

"What do you want to do, then?"

I decided, "Let us forbid Goli from ever entering our home. Let us forget that she ever existed."

A week later, the celebration of my wedding to Amir was trumpeted all over the city. When Goli arrived late, Amir's brother-in-law, Hossain, walked up to her and blocked her way. He turned around and gave her a little push back out the door. The last thing I heard was the applause and cheers of the others as Goli walked the walk of shame. From then on no one accepted a word Goli said.

Since then, I believe whole-heartedly that in the Roaring Twenties, not only the people in Paris broke with tradition, but we in Persia also dismantled some of our own rituals.

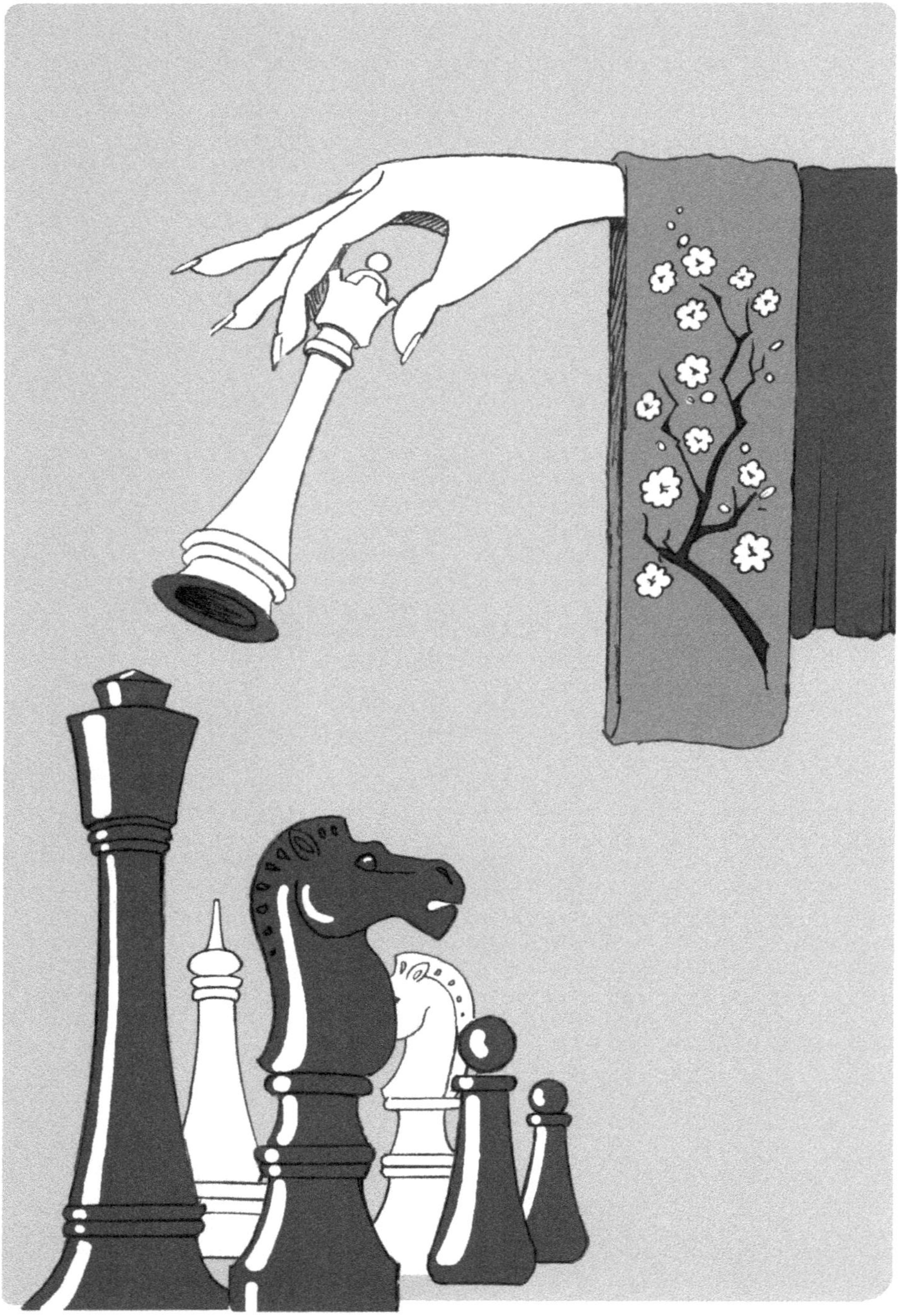

5. THE KING AND THE SHEPHERD'S DAUGHTER

*I don't know if you believe in reincarnation, but I do because
I have been reincarnated as a Persian girl many times.*

remember! Once, in the year fifteen fifty-five, I was in the body of a sixteen-year-old girl, called Neda. I lived with my father who was a shepherd in the outskirts of Isfahan, the capital of Persia, two hundred miles north of the Persian Gulf.

One day, I walked outside to catch a breath of fresh air when I saw several horsemen coming along the path in front of my tent. All of a sudden, I recognized the Majesty's coronet. To my surprise, he signaled the rest to stop. I didn't dare look him in the eyes. Instead, I bowed. With his kind words, he asked me for some water.

As if I were on fire, I ran inside and brought back his water in a blue bowl of baked clay—the best we had. While he was drinking, he never took his eyes away from me. "What's your name?"

"Neda, Your Majesty." I breathed.

"May I rest for a few minutes in your tent?"

"Your Majesty," I bowed again. "my father is not here and I'm alone. It is not advisable for me to let a stranger come in."

"All right!" The King's eyes beamed. He bade me farewell and rode off.

The rest of the day I was filled with joy at the experience of meeting our king— such a handsome and powerful man. Yet, I was also apprehensive about having rejected his wish to rest in my tent. *'Would he still be impressed by me?'*

That same evening, a man came to us. From outside our tent, he called for my father. I looked through the opening of the tent as my father stepped out. Without descending from his horse, the man shouted, "I am the King's advisor. His Majesty wants your daughter. Bring her out at once."

My father, who was known to have a quick temper, burst out with anger, "Hey you! I don't care who has sent you! My daughter is *not* a piece of cloth for the King to clean his hands with."

"Can't believe it," the stranger grumbled. "You, lowly shepherd! Aren't you pleased the King of Persia desires your daughter?"

Without answering him, my father walked back inside. The stranger shrugged, turned his horse, and went away.

The man's behavior was not honorable, yet I felt my heart fill with bliss. *'The Persian King fancies me!'*

The next day at noon, my father unexpectedly entered the tent. "Dear Neda, the King is asking for your hand! His Majesty's man is outside requesting to speak with you."

The nobleman entered the tent and addressed me. "Lady Neda! His Majesty requires of you three items."

"I'm all ears."

"First, please prepare one element that can be cooked in half without cooking the other half—keeping it as a unit. Second, spin half of one component without spinning the other part." He took a breath. "Third, weave something so that one portion of it stays unwoven."

"My Lord, why don't you rest as I prepare everything."

While His Majesty's man was resting, I instructed my father to butcher a male sheep. I cooked one of its testicles and put it in a dish along with the other uncooked one. I also spun part of its fleece and laid it in a dish with the other part not being spun. For the third item, I gathered some woolen thread to set on a loom in order to make a ball. I wove half of it and left the rest unwoven. At last I placed everything in a huge tray and covered it with a colorful silk handkerchief.

In addition, I cooked a dish with lamb shank mixed with saffron for the nobleman. As he ate it, he confessed that he had never had such a scrumptious dish before. He asked me to prepare a dish for the King as well. I presented him with a rack of lamb surrounded by fresh vegetables and fruits and decorated with wildflowers. Some of my father's boys carried the huge trays to the king's camp.

When the King's messenger arrived to alert me to prepare for the wedding, I dared to imagine myself as the queen of Persia living in Isfahan. I could barely swallow as the messenger went on to say, "The wedding will be at His Majesty's tent." In a moment, the bird of my imagination died along with my dreams. The King did not respect me enough to take me to his palace in the capital and marry me officially. I abhorred the idea of being added to His Majesty's harem.

It's true! A Moslem man was allowed to have four legal wives and numerous wives temporarily—from one hour, a week, a month, years, or for life. However, His Majesty's wives were kept in a harem for life. These women could not leave the harem or divorce their husband, the king, so that they might marry another man—normally a right for a Moslem woman. Even though I despised the thought that I would become His Majesty's concubine, I swallowed my fury.

On the wedding day, the nobleman and his guards came for me and my father. Like a sheep, I followed the entourage to His Majesty's camp. I then said "yes" to the Moslem priest after my father gave his permission. And so I was married to the King for life but not as his lawful wife and definitely not as his queen.

Before I was presented to him, two maids bathed me in luxurious goat milk. My long hair was also combed over and over and they dressed me in a shimmery white silk nightgown. Then, I was nudged into the King's tent.

His Majesty was tipsy. He filled his goblet with wine to the rim and sat upright in bed. "Come here Neda! Come and sit on my lap!"

"Yes, Your Majesty!" I took some hesitating steps toward the bed and sat at its edge with my back to him.

He tried to get close to me but I resisted. His Majesty finally lost his patience. "Refusing the King! Such an audacious move!"

"Forgive me, Your Majesty," I braved a possible storm. "I believe I deserve more."

"What did you say? More of what? Isn't it enough that I, the King of Persia, want to have you?"

"I'm honored, but…" I trailed off.

"But! What?" The King sounded irritated, unable to grab and hold on to me.

"Our country doesn't have a queen and I am worthy of being your queeeeeen!" I breathed.

"Queen of Persia? Such a whimsical desire!" He let out a laugh, "A shepherd's daughter wishes to be the queen of Persia… *ha ha!*" He turned over and passed out on the bed.

Before sunrise, I tiptoed outside without my shoes. My first thought was to take sanctuary in the forest. But I quickly dismissed this childish notion. During my morning prayers, I beseeched Allah to give me a chance to prove to the King that I was worthy of being his Queen.

The following morning, the King's men took down the king's hunting camp and we set out for the palace in Isfahan. When we arrived, I was immediately sent to the harem. I believed His Majesty would forget all about me, especially for refusing him on our wedding night.

After a few weeks, to my surprise, the King called me to his presence. "Neda!"

"Your Majesty!" I bowed.

"If you want to be my queen," the King said, "you must prove that you are the wisest woman of the land."

"Yes, Your Majesty!" I perked up at the challenge. "I will indeed prove to you that I am worthy of being your queen."

The King arose and put several bedazzling jewels in a box. He then took the royal seal made of red wax and embossed with a lion at the bottom, over to the candle flame and sealed the box shut. "Tomorrow morning, I am going away for a year. When I come back, I want to find stones instead of jewels in this box with its seal unbroken." He walked when he pointed outside, "Those two horses are my favorite ones. I will take the stallion with me. The mare must get pregnant by that same stallion." He then ordered two slaves to be brought in—one male and one female. "I will take the male with me. The female stays with you and must get pregnant by the male slave."

He stared into my eyes as he went on, "Above all, when I see you again at the end of the year, you must also have a baby and you must prove to me that the infant is mine. If all these things aren't executed the way I have ordered, you will be thrown out of the palace in disgrace."

"I accept all challenges, Your Majesty," I exclaimed.

I had no idea how to solve these seemingly impossible tasks. That night I stayed up thinking and praying until I devised a plan.

My innate kindness had won the respect and loyalty of the harem eunuchs. So, when I asked a few I had chosen for their help, they were more than happy to go along with my strategy. They pledged an oath of secrecy after I promised to reward them handsomely. Together, we assembled what was needed to carry out my plan.

The next morning I learned that the King and his men had left the palace. I dressed in the costume of a Chinese prince, took the box of jewels, the mare and the female slave. The seven eunuchs, in their Chinese uniforms with helmets and visors covering their faces, mounted their horses. My company rode fast along a shorter route so that we arrived ahead of His Majesty at the lush hunting grounds where I ordered my companions to encamp.

Upon my instructions, we pretended that I was a Chinese prince who had come to Persia for hunting. I knew this would not raise any suspicion because at that time a strong trade relationship existed between the two countries. We loved Chinese silk and the Chinese were attached to our rugs and spices. The passage between our two countries was known as, "The Silk Road."

The following day, the King and his escorts arrived. Shortly after, one of my men announced that the Persian King's guard was here to see me—the Chinese Prince. He entered my tent, bowed and invited me to be His Majesty's guest for that night.

I lowered my voice an octave replying, "I gladly accept the Majesty's invitation."

As the sun sank down into the West, I went to the King's camp accompanied by my guards. The Persian King welcomed me warmly, offering me a seat by his side on a jeweled throne. We engaged in light conversation. Before dinner was served, as was the King's habit, he and I played a game of chess. The King was surprised that he won it so quickly and, thus, was happy when I requested to play another game, this time with a bet—the King's stallion versus my mare.

We started to play. This time, I handily checkmated the King and won his horse. Dinner time arrived—no time for more chess that night, and upon finishing the meal, I asked permission to leave.

Even though the King loved his stallion, he sent it over to my camp where I had ordered the stallion to be put in with the mare.

At dawn, one of my guards, again wearing a helmet covering his face, took the stallion back to the King's camp. The guard returned and informed me that the King's desire was to come for a visit to my tent.

This night, we bet the King's male slave against my female slave. Again, I pronounced "checkmate". After His Majesty left the tent, his favorite slave was brought to me and I ordered him placed together with the female slave.

The next morning the male slave was sent back to the King's camp. At night, the King invited me to his tent again. The King's seal versus my seal was our bet. And, once again, I, the Chinese Prince, defeated the Persian King. I took the seal and left.

When I arrived at my own camp, I broke the seal to the box, took out the jewels, and replaced them with river rocks of the same weight. Then I closed the box and sealed it with red wax the same way it had been. In the morning, I sent the seal back to the King along with an additional note thanking His Majesty for trusting me with his seal.

Once more, in the evening, we played chess as we had on every other night. This time the bet was if the King won, I would give him my Chinese female slave. If I won, the King would pay all the expenses of my hunting trip. On this night, I deliberately lost the game to the King. After we ate, the King left the tent.

I took off the costume I was wearing as the Chinese prince. I mixed some flour in water and smeared it on my face including my eyelids so that my olive skin appeared much lighter. I blended a bit of pulverized ink with water and using a calligraphy pen made of bamboo I drew delicate lines around my eyelids giving them an oriental appearance. I tied my hair up and decorated it with Chinese ornaments. By the time I slipped into a colorful silk brocade Kimono, my work was complete. I resembled a China doll just arrived from the Silk Road. When I walked out, even some of my own guards stared at me as if they had never seen such a beautiful Chinese woman before.

I called on two of my men to escort me to the King's camp. The moment His Majesty cast a glance at me, he was mesmerized by my irresistible exquisiteness. We spent the entire night together making love. But as a Moslem man, the Persian King had forgotten an important rule of Islam: "No man shall get close to a woman unless he marries her first."

When the sun rose, the King said, "China Doll! I feel obligated to return you to the Prince, even though I do not wish to." He looked sad. "My generosity is not less than a Chinese Prince."

I pretended I had no idea what he was talking about!

So, it was with a heavy heart, the Persian King let me go.

Back at my camp, I instructed my servants to prepare for our departure. That evening, I, the Chinese prince, requested of the King that we spend this last night away from our respective camps.

The King and I spent a pleasant evening at the riverbank without playing any games or betting. Due to my encouragement, the King drank wine much more than I did. Soon, he fell into a deep sleep. In the middle of the night, I tiptoed away. My men and I galloped until early the next morning when we reached Isfahan.

The King stayed away for the rest of the year. At last he returned to the palace. He went to his room where he saw a cradle awaiting him. He called for me demanding, "Whose baby is this?"

I bowed and gestured. "It is your male slave's, your Majesty. Your mare also delivered a colt last night from *your* stallion to which the royal groom will testify." A servant then brought the box, bowed, and put it before the King. The seal appeared untouched. By the King's order, the box was opened. He gazed flummoxed at the rocks in the place of jewels. The King shook his head in amazement. "How did you solve these riddles?"

Proudly I replied, "Your Majesty, remember the days you spent hunting, getting to know the Chinese Prince, and the nights playing chess?"

"Yes…"

I took out my princely disguise and showed it to the King. He gasped, "Oh… You were the Chinese Prince!"

I nodded. "And the Chinese slave girl!"

The King could only stand there with his mouth agape.

"Your Majesty, you must have forgotten one piece of the puzzle—the most important one, if I may say so." I snapped my fingers and a nursemaid walked in the room, carrying a swaddled baby. Without a word, the maid put the infant in the King's arms, bowed and departed.

"Meet your son, Majesty," I beamed with delight. The King looked into the baby's eyes. He murmured in awe, "He looks just like me!"

Acknowledging my extraordinary wisdom, the King bowed to me. I had proven to His Majesty that I was the wisest woman in Persia.

The King married me officially in an elaborate palace ceremony. He commanded that there be a celebration of our wedding throughout the country for seven days and nights.

And that's how *I*, a poor shepherd's daughter, became the Queen of Persia.

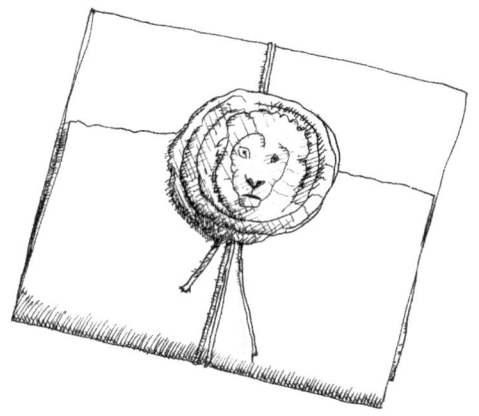

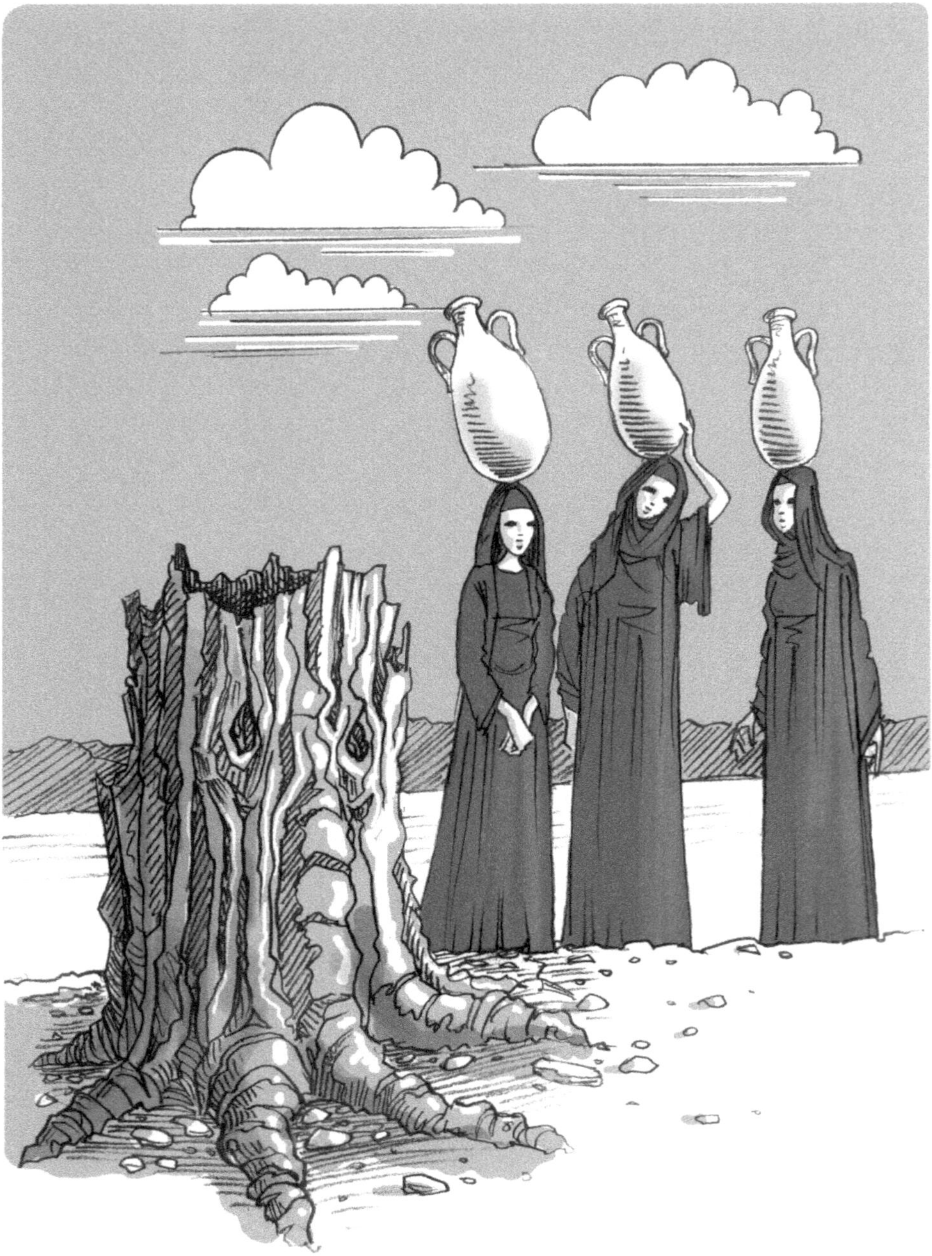

6. THE STORY OF COURAGEOUS BIBI

*I don't know if you believe in reincarnation, but I do because
I have been reincarnated as a Persian girl many times.*

remember! Once in the thirteenth century, I occupied the body of a fourteen-year-old girl. My name was Bibi and I lived with my parents in a village called Baft. It was in the southeast of Persia, five hundred miles from the border of Afghanistan.

Every day I fetched water with two friends from a spring which passed nearby to an old tree stump. One day while the three of us were filling up our jugs, we heard a gravely voice which appeared to be coming from the stump, "Not the follower, not the one in the middle, but the one ahead!" The voice nailed all of us down. "Tell your mother to bring to me soon what she has promised me."

My friends were petrified. One of them asked, "Which one of us are you referring to?"

"The voice didn't mean me." I responded daringly and changed my place from the head to the middle to see what would happen.

"Not the first, not the last," The stump spoke again, "but the middle one! Your mother gave her word to me. Remind her!"

I was a bit unnerved. I quickly switched my place with the girl at the end. Once more the stump spoke, "Not the first, not the middle, but the last one! Tell your mother she needs to follow through on what she vowed to me."

I urged my friends to ignore the voice and we took our water and went home. Anxiously, I asked my mother, "What kind of agreement do you have with the stump? A voice coming from it keeps telling me to remind you of your pledge!"

My mother lowered her head. As a young woman, she could not have any children. She had wanted so badly to have a child that, out of desperation, she solemnly promised her firstborn to the stump. "The time has come." With sadness she continued, "I must now give you over to the stump."

She covered my head, gave me an old mat and some food. She took my hand, and we walked to the stump. She was crying all the way. She spread the mat next to it and told me to sit. "You must do whatever the voice asks of you." While she was wiping her tears, she said. "From now on you are maid to this stump."

She walked away while her moaning and wailing filled the entire land.

Being an obedient daughter, I stayed by the stump. At night I began to shiver for it was the onset of winter. A short while later, I heard a deafening rumble and became frightened. I could do nothing. I was frozen motionless like a rock. The thundering sound came again even louder.

This time, I responded. "Stump! Are you genie, fairy, or demon? Whatever you are, please show yourself to me."

To my surprise, a kind voice came out of the stump. "I'm not a fairy or genie. You shouldn't be afraid of me. Trust me."

Ignoring my loud heart beating, I stood up. When I looked down, a large hole had opened up in the middle of the stump. I could tell it was just my size. A tremendous urge overcame me to discover the man behind the voice. And I needed to get out of the cold air as well. So, after reciting a verse of the Koran for protection, I closed my eyes, and stepped into the open space in the stump.

Magically, I found myself in a huge house set in a lush forest. Wall-to-wall beautiful and colorful carpets covered each room. Out of thin air, a huge wooden chest emerged. Instinctively, I opened its door. I could not believe my eyes! It was full of colorful, expensive clothes.

I felt quite grateful at the appearance of a furnace. As I warmed my hands, a handsome young man came into view. His majestic look—like a prince, attracted me.

He entered the house and approached me. In the same kind voice I had heard while sitting by the stump. He spoke, "I am Morad, a nobleman." He gestured all around him. "This is the magical land of

Shush." He cast an admiring look at me and continued. "From the time I was a little boy, I always knew you would someday appear. And now, here you are." A smile lit up his dapper face.

In spite of being bewildered by this magical land, I realized he was proposing to me. Our eyes met. I felt a strong love for him. Morad bowed to me and formally asked, "Will you marry me?"

I was surprised. This nobleman knew that in Islam, the bride-to-be had to utter her acceptance to the marriage. "Yes!" I replied.

Morad pulled a turquoise ring from his pocket and put it on my finger. "With this ring, I marry you. You're my wife now and this is our house."

I eagerly pledged my devotion to him as my husband for the rest of my life.

He then took the opulent white fur garment from his back. He gave it to me and said, "As my wife, take good care of this cloak. It's magical. If one day you lose or destroy it, you and I will be separated."

All of my previous doubts and fears were replaced by joy and love for Morad. I assured him, "I'll safeguard this, making sure nothing happens to it."

Early the next morning, Morad left our house to go hunting. I heard a knock at our door. When I opened it, I saw a well-dressed lady who greeted me kindly. She claimed she was Morad's aunt, Aafat. I felt uncommonly close to her as if she was my own aunt. All day, we drank tea, ate sweets and chatted. I was amazed that she knew a lot about my tiny village of Baft. Before leaving, she said, "Dear Bibi, promise me you'll keep my visit a secret between the two of us. No need for Morad to know."

"Why not, dear Aafat?"

"He and I had a dispute...got to go!" And she dashed out.

I had no idea why but sensed I was compelled to keep her visit a secret.

Each day, Aafat came for a visit right after my husband left home. I was pleased not to be alone during the day. Even though I loved Morad and had a fabulous life, I was still missing my family. It seemed like Aafat read the sorrow in my face. One day she said, "Dear Bibi, you must be tired of your life; not having any company besides me."

"I don't have any other choice," I explained. "My mother pledged me to the stump."

"Would you like me to help you go back to your family?"

"No, It's my fate to be away from my mother. I obey Allah's will whole heartedly."

The next day, Aafat came for lunch with a small bowl of *aash*, my favorite thick soup. She did not eat any of it. I loved it so much that I gobbled all of it. Not long after that I felt the whole house spinning and couldn't remember anything else. When I finally woke up, I found myself back on my old mat, wearing my old ragged clothes. There was no sign of the fur garment and no mansion. *Poof! Everything was gone.* With tears in my eyes, I concluded that Aafat had brought this misfortune upon me. I set out to see my mother. I told her of my journey as I showed her the only thing I had left from Morad — the turquoise ring. "Dear Mama, I am going to look for my husband."

"My dear child," my mother replied with a heavy heart, "you have no idea where to look for him!"

"I must go! The Almighty as my guide, I will find him." I hugged her goodbye and I went back to the stump. I prayed for quite some time until an opening appeared to me. I stepped into it.

Instead of Morad's mansion and beautiful forests, this time a bleak desert stretched out before me. There was no way I could let the shock of the desolated land frighten me.

I had no idea exactly how many days and nights I walked the bare lands or how many times I fell down on the sand dunes. With parched lips and scorched feet, I kept praying Allah to guide me while keeping the fire of Morad's love in my heart.

At last, I came to a flock of sheep near an oasis. The shepherd had a hunchback and two small horns on his head amidst his mangled hair. His appearance was startling, especially when I found the third eye in the middle of his forehead staring at me. However, I overcame my aversion and called to him, "Mister! Please spare me some milk."

"Go away, woman," the wretched shepherd snorted. "These sheep belong to our leader, Morad, and his wife, Bibi. I don't have permission…"

"I'm Bibi!"

His hideous laugh shook me to my core. "Outrageous!" He howled. "Nobody knows what happened to her and strangers aren't welcome here."

Without knowing how to prove my identity, I continued on my way until I came to a herd of camel tended by a disfigured man identical in appearance to the shepherd. I mustered up my courage and addressed him, "I am Bibi. Let me have some milk." The same rebuke as from the first deformed cowherd filled my ears.

I was discouraged but proceeded on my way until I arrived at a gushing spring of clear water. Soon, I sighted a young boy with a jug in his hand coming up to the same stream of water. I was amazed by his look. He was a normal young lad in black trousers and long garment. By his white turban, I discerned he had to be a servant to an important family. "Hey!" I cried out, "I'm thirsty. May I have some water from your jug?"

"I'm sorry," The boy said with regret, "This water belongs to Master Morad and I have no permission to share it with anyone else."

I cursed from the bottom of my heart. "May the water turn into blood!"

The boy shrugged and set out on his way.

After a short while, the boy returned. I took my turquoise ring off my finger and put it in my mouth before the boy was near me.

"Here! Drink as much as you want. Are you a witch or something?" He gulped. "Master Morad gave me permission to let you have some water." He extended the jug to me.

I poured the blood out, filled the pitcher with the spring water. I took it to my lips and as I did so, I spit the ring into it. After drinking the last drop, I filled it with fresh water and gave it back to the servant.

Soon after, I detected Morad close to me. I had an urge to run to him, embrace him, and apologize for keeping a secret from him. But the look in his eyes nailed me to my spot. "Lady!" He called as if he didn't know me. "What are you doing here?" Then he handed me a sack and whispered, "You've entered into the land of demons."

"Yes, they look hideous!" I murmured.

"Aafat, the sorceress, put a black spell on these people and their land."

"The same spell which caused our separation," I said.

Morad gave me a head signal. "Aafat is not my aunt," He said under his breath, "she stole me from my parents as a baby and brought me to this land. She changed all the people of Shush into Demons with her evil black powder—except a few of them intended to be our servants. After raising me, Aafat commissioned me to be in charge of these creatures."

"So sorry!"

"I'm under her spell too!" Morad frowned. "The only thing that kept me safe was the magic fur. It had the ability to keep her devilish force at bay." He paused. "But since it's gone, Aafat's black magic is once again in full force."

"No wonder Aafat pursued me so eagerly—to get a hold of the fur," I sighed. "But now that I've found you, we must find a way to overcome her."

"My house is a long way from here. Continue on your way, and meet me there. But you must pretend we don't know each other." In the blink of an eye, he disappeared.

After seeing Morad, I realized how much I loved him. I was even more determined to return to the wonderful life I had shared with him. So that Aafat would not recognize me, I put some mud on my hair and made it stay upright and rigid in two prongs to look like horns. I smudged some of the mud on my face too. Then I rolled in the dirt to make my clothes look bedraggled.

When I arrived at the same mansion where Morad and I had lived for a while, I knocked. A servant opened the door.

"I've travelled a long way. May I stop here to rest?" I implored.

The servant went in to the house, and Morad came to the door. He covered my head and face with a see-through cloth and took me to Aafat's quarters. "This poor girl is lost. Why don't we hire her as my maid?"

What do you want a maid for?" Aafat queried.

But Morad insisted. At last, Aafat agreed although with hesitation added, "She must come at nights to my quarter to sleep. I know she's a human," she shrilled.

"Yes, she is! Remember, here in Shush besides you and I all our servants are also humans."

They went back and forth for some time until Aafat, who did not recognize me, reluctantly accepted the arrangement. Morad took me to his quarters as his maid.

In the middle of the night, I met Morad in the hallway. We quietly planned our escape. I revealed to him that during my prayers, I had a vision of what we would need to run away. I instructed him to groom his horse. I took several bags of salt from the kitchen and met him in the stable.

We mounted the horse immediately. I held on to Morad's waist as we fled.

In the dusk that followed, I looked over my shoulder and caught a glimpse of Aafat from far away. "How can she reach us?" I asked Morad.

"Aafat, the sorceress, has the ability to propel herself inches off the ground at a fantastic speed. She never tires!" Morad sped on. "Her black magic also gives her enhanced vision. She is able to follow the hoof prints of the horse to track us down."

Desperately, I started praying to Allah, Morad also started reciting verses of the Koran with me. As Aafat approached, I emptied the bags of salt all around us while I beseeched Allah. Magically, the salt became a sea. Morad and I easily crossed this shallow sea with our horse.

Aafat knew that getting wet with salt water would be fatal to her. She screeched, "Hey Morad, my son! Help me! How can I cross the sea?"

"She thinks," Morad whispered to me. "I'm still under her spell."

"I'm so pleased, my love," I murmured, "you are far from her and by reciting the verses of the Koran, you are safe."

Morad shouted, "To come over, just step onto that large shiny white rock."

She believed him and jumped to step on the rock that was in reality the reflection of the moon. As she sunk into the sea, Morad and I heard her shrieks. *Poof!* She disappeared in the salt water.

Neither one of us noticed the wave that splashed on to the shore. All we saw was a gazelle standing by the edge of the salt sea. After the effort of the escape, Morad suddenly realized how hungry he was. He decided the gazelle would be a delicious meal and started to stalk it.

But the four-legged creature was unafraid, as if tamed. Morad did not have the heart to kill it. "Why don't we take this harmless animal home?" He looked at me. "It can be a good company for you."

"Now that we're far from Shush and Aafat is gone," I breathed a sigh of relief. "let's do that."

Each day when Morad went hunting, I stayed with the gazelle. As soon as we were alone, the creature began butting me with its head or kicking me in the stomach. But the moment Morad would returned, the gazelle became its adorable self again.

After a few weeks of this, I had no other choice but to complain to my husband, "We need to get rid of this gazelle. When you're not here, it becomes vicious, ramming and striking me."

"You don't mean this tame faun?" remarked Morad in disbelief.

In the middle of that very same night, I opened my eyes and saw Morad in a death-like trance. I jumped up and there was Aafat, pointing out the window to the backyard. "Come with me," she commanded.

"Where is the gazelle?" I looked hard and long at Aafat and realized that she had transformed herself into the gazelle.

"I am throwing you in that pot. I want to hear your screams while you die an agonizing death." Aafat uttered.

While I was shaking Morad in hopes of waking him, I could smell the smoke and heard the sound of boiling water. I was shouting through my tears, "What did you do to my husband?"

"I'm afraid he's dead," cackled Aafat. "The only way to save your husband is to sacrifice yourself. Your life for his!"

"I'd do anything for my beloved Morad." I followed Aafat outside. Through my tears I uttered, "Now that I'm going to die, grant me my last wish."

"What is it?" Aafat snapped with impatience.

"Allow me to pray to Allah three units of prayers…then do whatever you want to do with me."

She hesitated and nodded, "Make it quick!"

I climbed the ladder to the roof to pray. When I got to my last prayer, tears were cascading down my face. *Behold!* An angel appeared before me.

"Do not cry," she addressed me, "your husband is not dead. Aafat has put his soul in a bottle. It is on the shelf downstairs. Break the bottle, so he'll wake up and the two of you together can overcome the sorceress."

Before I could utter a word, she disappeared.

I dried my tears and went down the ladder where I found Aafat giddy with excitement at the prospect of boiling me to death. I said, "Let me kiss my husband goodbye."

She followed me inside, grumbling under her breath. I kissed Morad on the cheek then turned to Aafat, "Now, I'm ready to meet Allah. Lead the way."

Aafat eagerly headed for the boiling pot. She had just reached the doorway when I pushed her from behind, I gave the sorceress a hard shove out the door, then quickly slammed it shut and locked it. I hurried to the shelf, grabbed the bottle, and smashed it to the floor.

The bottle exploded in a cloud of dust. Moments later, Morad awoke from the sleeping spell and we rushed into each other's arms.

When Aafat realized her plot had been foiled, she changed herself back into the gazelle again.

Morad and I went outside where he noticed the pot in the middle of the yard. He asked, "What's the boiling water for?"

"For me! Aafat prepared it to kill me." I pointed to the gazelle.

Without hesitation, Morad picked up the animal and dropped it into the pot. We could not ignore her loud scream. "Thank Allah! Aafat is dead for good!"

"No! It's not over yet," Morad gasped. "Didn't you see some water splashed out? As soon as it hit the ground, a drop transformed into a crow and flew away?"

"Really!" In distrust, I said. "How could I miss that?"

"Aafat is still very much alive." Morad caressed my hair, "She breathes evil air and can change into any form or shape."

I shook my head in frustration. "Is there any way we can get rid of her and her spell for good?"

"Yes, but it won't be easy," exclaimed Morad.

"How can we get rid of her?"

"It'd be the most difficult journey you've ever made…" declared Morad.

"For a peaceful life without Aafat, I'll do anything." I was decisive.

"The sad part is I can't come with you," Morad said regretfully.

"I know." I uttered, "As soon as she sees you, she'll unleash one of her spells on you."

"Dear Bibi! Allah has sent you to break her spell for good." He took my hands in his. "Listen carefully. You must travel to Aafat's fortress where she goes to restore her powers after they have been weakened."

"I'll go to wherever she is." My voice was assertive.

Morad went on. "She has many maids, so many she can't recall their names. You can disguise yourself as one of them to get close to her." He continued explaining to me that there was a small urn that contained magic white powder. "It belonged to my parents," Morad's face turned sad. "But, before they could use it on her, Aafat killed them. She took the urn and fled to Shush."

"What did she do with it?"

"She hid it from me. But, when I was in a death-like trance, I saw she'd hidden it under her pillow where she was resting."

"What do I do with the powder when I get hold of it?"

"My dear, you must throw it in her face," said Morad. "This will neutralize her black magic and she will be stripped of her witchcraft."

"I'm ready to get rid of this wicked woman." I was serious and sincere. Right away, I set out on my journey in search of Aafat's fortress.

After many days and nights in the desert, I noticed a citadel in the distance made of dark wood with many dried tree trunks rising high into the sky surrounding the residence, shielding it from the eyes of any intruder. The walls were covered with sharp wooden spikes. The gate, however, was made of a smooth shiny wood. I ignored my trembling hands and knocked. No answer came but the door cracked open. I understood that every maid was under Aafat's spell. Whenever she needed anyone, she would simply awaken one of them.

When I entered the yard, the eerie silence unnerved me tremendously. In one corner, I saw a haggard black bulldog that had straw before it. On the other side was a gaunt camel with a pile of bones in front of it. I felt sorry for them. I switched the straw and bones and was rewarded at the sight of animals happily chewing on the foods meant for them.

Before entering the main house, I covered my face with a scarf except for my eyes. In search of Aafat, I went along the hall to the first room. I opened the door and saw a soiled carpet and bed. I pretended to be a maid, cleaning and arranging them neatly. Then I opened a huge door where I saw Aafat, lying down on her bed. All of a sudden, she sat up straight and ordered, "Come here and brush my hair." She handed me a wooden comb. I obeyed.

"Put your head on my lap," I said kindly when I sat behind her. The pillow with the white magic urn underneath was between me and her body.

"When did you get here?" She sniffed my underarm. "You smell new to me."

I ignored her comment and continued brushing every wisp of her hair while singing lullabies to her until she fell into a deep sleep. I slipped my right hand under the pillow and stealthily took out the white urn while combing her hair with the other. I quickly removed the cork with my teeth and splashed its white powder on her face.

Aafat couldn't help but inhale the powder. She jerked upright and tried to cough and spit it out but to no avail. Her face contorted and swelled, turning a shade of green, then red, then blue. At last it became a stark white like the powder itself.

She jumped out of bed, reached into her robe and moved a fistful of black powder to throw on me. But the evil powder burned her hand like acid. Her power had lost its diabolical effect. Some of the white powder landed on the mattress releasing it from her spell, and turning it back into the huge slave it had been before.

Aafat screeched, "Human grab the girl!"

The man did not move. "Why should I?" he said calmly. "She's done me no harm. You, on the other hand, have laid on me with your filthy body for seven years."

I let out a big sigh and left the room in no hurry.

Aafat was still believing in her sorcery. She followed me outside to the yard and ordered the camel, "Hold the girl with your teeth."

"Why?" Answered the camel. "You gave me bones for seven years. She gave me straw right away."

She then commanded the dog, "Bite the girl!"

"Why should I?" the dog replied, "You put straw before me for seven years, she gave me bones; if biting is good, let me bite you." The dog attacked her and tore Aafat's body apart, from limb to limb.

Her death screams reminded me Aafat had wanted to hear my wailing by throwing me into the boiling water. While the dog was tearing her apart, it was my time to hear her screaming in agony, loud and clear.

I stepped out in triumph, knowing for sure that the wicked witch Aafat was dead and gone, once and for all. I headed for the village. As I got close, I heard what sounded like celebration. And when I walked down the main street, a raucous round of cheers went up. I was swarmed by the villagers who were no longer demons, returned to their human form with the death of Aafat. They hoisted me on their shoulders and carried me over to Morad, laughing and singing all the while. When Morad and I embraced and kissed, another round of cheers went up. We returned to the original mansion and lived under the Smile of Allah for many years to come.

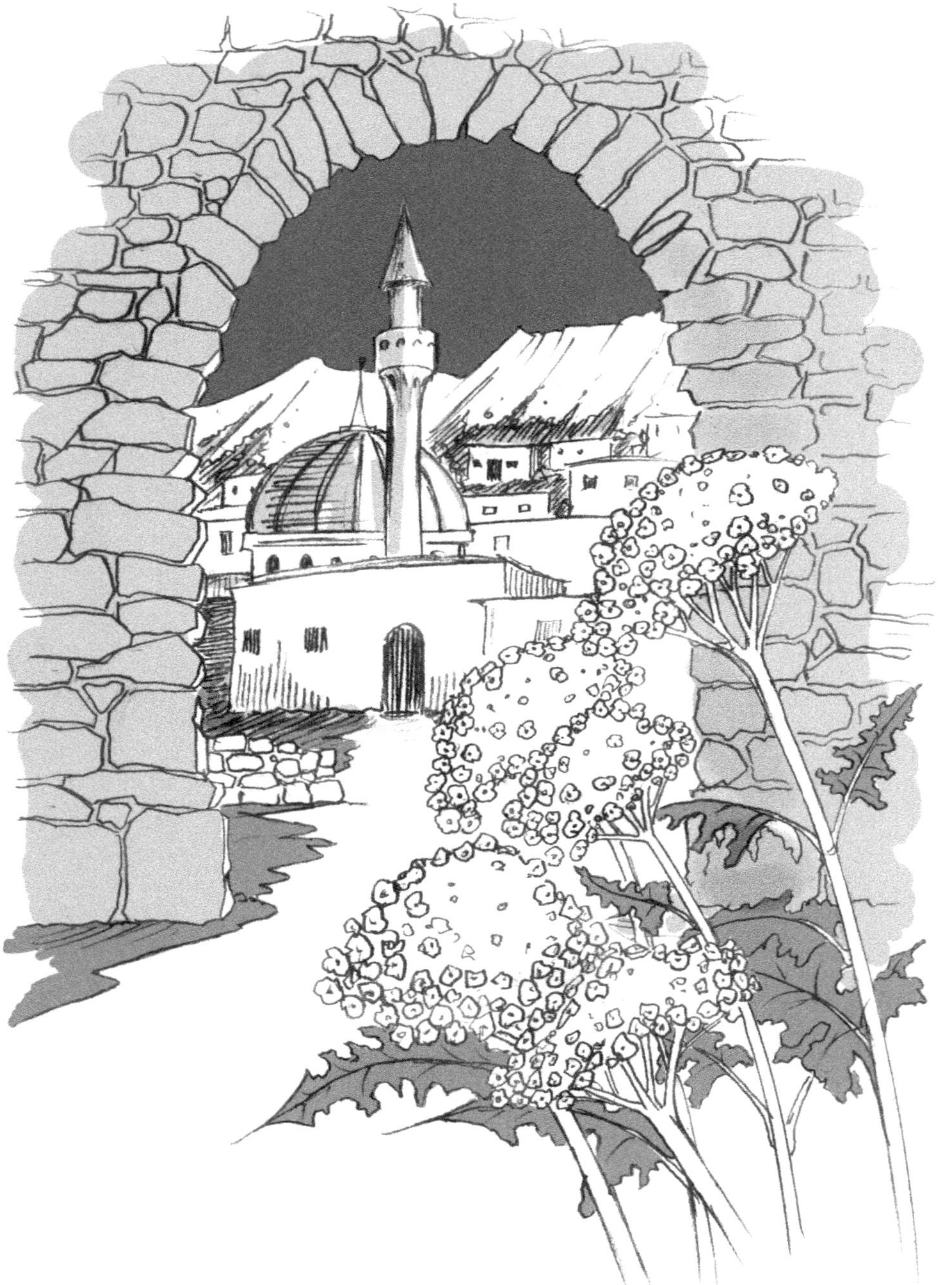

7. YARROW —
THE FLOWER OF MOTHER'S SWEET
SCENT

*I don't know if you believe in reincarnation, but I do because
I have been reincarnated as a Persian girl many times.*

remember! Once at the end of the eighteenth century, I was a
thirty-year-old woman living in Shahreza, a village seven hundred miles south of Tehran, the capital of Persia. No one knew
my given name. Almost all of the two hundred villagers loved
me so much that they gave me the title of "the Matron" which means
an angel sent by God to take care of them. Or maybe the name was
given to me because of my heavenly aroma that lingered in the room
long after I had gone. Some wondered whether it was a perfume I used.
Some believed it was the mixed scent of Nature with that of Love.

There was only one purpose in my life—to help others.

I got up every day before sunrise but not to pray like the rest of the
Moslems. Instead, I would complete my household tasks at home and
then devote the rest of my time to do other undertakings for the villagers. I would spin cotton. From its threads I stitched garments for
the poor residents. I made oil from castor beans to light up all the lamps
in the village. I was able to churn cream, butter and cheese from the
milk of my few goats and share it with everyone. Because of the absence
of a doctor in our village, I assisted women giving birth. Sometimes, I
also boiled herbs and spices to heal a child's tummy ache. Whatever I
cooked was the talk of our village. I fed the hungry with plates heaped
with fluffy rice covered with saffron and legs of chicken basted in
turmeric and tomato juice. Their voices of admiration filled the air.
"Allah Bless You!" "Long Live our Matron."

When my only daughter, Tooba turned five, my husband suddenly
died. After forty days of mourning for him, I assumed his duties in addition to mine. I went to the forests and with his axe cut firewood.

Whenever it was needed, I repaired my cottage. Because I knew how to ride a horse and shoot a gun, I went hunting just like my late husband. Thus, thieves and robbers would think twice about getting close to me or my hut. On the farm, I plowed, planted, harvested the crops and divided most of them among the destitute.

I worked all day long but this created discord between the farmers and their wives. "See! The Matron does not ever take a break," one of the wives sneered, as she put his lunch down in front of her husband.

Another wife asked in a contemptuous voice, "What kind of a man are you?"

As they ate their lunches and smoked their pipes, the men complained, "Why can't she do only the woman's work like other women and not meddle in men's affairs."

I turned a deaf ear to the grumbling. I kept on working, producing an abundance and donating almost all to the poor ones.

At Tooba's twentieth birthday though, I began to slow down. Over the years I became weaker and weaker until I was bed ridden. When my end was near, I called on her, "Dear Tooba…" I could barely breathe, "you need to know…soon I'll become a plant with pretty flowers…spreading sweet aroma."

"But Mama, a seed ought to be planted first before having a flower!" Tooba exclaimed.

"Well," I agreed, "like a seed planted in the spring…I'll also grow into a plant and bloom." I took a labored breath. "Of course…I'll show you the place for it. Promise me once in a while you'll come there…where I'm resting. You will see me as yellow flowers with a beautiful sweet smell." I swallowed. "I assure you…after seeing those flowers… you'll love them. And when you smell them, they will be a reminder of *me*."

When my end was near, the villagers gathered around me, crying and saying their goodbyes. Tooba's dried eyes were peaceful. *And that pleased me the most!*

After my death, Tooba came to the cemetery every week rain or shine, but saw no sign of my return. She grew impatient and cried out, "Mama where are you? I came to take you home!" I could only answer her in silence.

Weeks turned into months. One day, in the following spring, as Tooba was approaching the cemetery, all of a sudden she shouted elatedly, "Mama! Are you back?" She took a deep breath and continued, "Our land's immersed in your *scent!*" As she ran toward my grave, she found it was covered with yellow flowers. She picked some, smelled them, and murmured, "Indeed, it's a mixture of Nature and Love."

She then carried the flowers to the village. Before the villagers could even see her, they cheered, "Is our Matron back? We smell her fragrance —the same heavenly aroma." Then, they saw Tooba with the yellow flowers.

Ever since, in Shahreza, the villagers have known yarrow as a flower of a mother's sweet scent!

Nowadays, whenever you go to a mall in this country, make sure to go inside the French perfume store, L'Occitane (LOX-EE-TAN) and inhale their fragrance. It is made of yarrow, or mother's sweet scent. Then you would know what angels smell like.

CONCLUSION

In these stories we live vicariously through a Persian girl who rein-carnates at different times during the history of Persia and faces adver-sity in each of her lives. She encounters two opposite forces—Good and Evil. She learns that sometimes it is impossible for good to win over evil right away. However, she never loses her convictions. The heroine seeks help or guidance over and over from God, Allah, the most powerful sources of Goodness for her. By abiding and following His path, she comes to happiness and is ultimately rewarded for her efforts.

Obviously, fairy tales are far from ordinary life. Yet, the fact remains —in our lives these two opposing forces exist—one coin with two faces. We need not only be aware of this truth in order to make better choices in our own lives but also to teach our children to live with these polar oppositions perhaps helping them to overcome some harmful situa-tions.

These fables teach us that the world consists of conflicts between many opposing forces—morality and corruption; material and spiri-tual; beauty and ugliness. These stories also advance our awareness not to be fooled by the materialistic world. Being aware of these divergent forces enables us to be conscientious individuals.

It is clear that from childhood we learn to distinguish between these two conflicting dynamics—Right and Wrong. It reminds me of a re-mark my three-year-old grandson made when he was telling me how he sat quietly at the salon for the lady to cut his hair for the first time, even though he hated the whole affair. He said giggling, "Aziz, I was thinking about hitting the lady and running out of there. But, I didn't. We don't do that! Hurting someone is no good!"

We live by the rule of choosing light over darkness, learning to listen to our inner voice. It is our duty not to ignore this dichotomy. Instead, we need to accept these two polarities in our lives, no matter where we are from. As the twentieth century mythologist, Joseph Campbell (1904 - 1987 AD), has taught us—to disregard these conflicts within ourselves or in our lives as valueless would be an important loss to our humanity.

You have likely found many similarities among these tales and Western tales. One of the most notable resemblances is that, most of the time, stories from the East or West have a happy ending. Yet, there is one important difference. In Western culture, the main character, or hero, returns home triumphant from his quest and then as his reward, he marries his love and 'they live happily ever after.' However, in six out of seven of these sample stories from Persia, the protagonists, the female characters, marry fairly soon after the beginning of the tale. In order to achieve a fulfilling life, each goes through several odysseys before finding her happiness, with the exception of the heroine in "Yarrow —The Flower of Mother's Sweet Scent". For the Matron, death is the ultimate happiness, even though, she still keeps an eye on her daughter.

My greatest hope is that you—specifically the young adults—take these stories to heart and mind. That you are successful in your life is my utmost desire. Sadly not many contemporary works have endured and explored the universal issues that youth must experience on their road to maturity. I believe that educating our youth about other cultures, is a step forward to seeking a peaceful solution to the turmoil of today's world.

LITERARY ANALYSIS
LAND OF ROSES AND NIGHTINGALES

In the history of humankind, folktales and fairytales have played a major role because they are the origin of any literary works. Yet their importance was never fully recognized until the twentieth century. As modern psychology gained prominence, some scholars such as Carl Jung in *Man and his Symbols*, and Joseph Campbell in *The Hero with a Thousand Faces,* came to the conclusion that, since every human mind is created the same way, the pattern of the mind and its productions are likely to be the same everywhere. This theory is known as "Collective Unconscious". In other words, what man has told us as tales in the past resembles what he is writing as fiction in the present. Jung believes that the primitive man everywhere has produced the "hero myth". According to Jung, the hero has some general traits like "humble birth, his early proof of superhuman strength, his rapid rise to prominence or power, his triumphant struggle with the forces of evil…." These seven stories would provide proof of Jung's theory.

Much of modern psychology sees the conflict between hero and evil forces as the struggle of primitive man to achieve higher consciousness. Campbell explains in *The Hero with a Thousand Faces* that, "The hero… is the man or woman who has been able to battle…[her] personal and local historical limitations to the generally valid, normally human forms." Interestingly, the same idea is the foundation of the ancient Persian religion, Zoroastrianism.

Extensive exploration in Greek or Roman mythology reveals that a female hero as protagonist can seldom be found. Only during the last several centuries have male heroes been occasionally replaced by females. Some authors such as Jane Austen, Virginia Wolf, Alice Walker and Suzanne Collins reinstated young female characters in their successful novels; even though their genres are very different from fairytales. These women portray their conflicts and challenges in life, just like their male counter-parts. These heroes seek adventures, solve riddles and use their wisdom to create the ultimate happiness for their community and themselves. As we witness, in *Hunger Games* the older sister saves her younger sister's life by coming forward in place of her to be part of the dangerous games.

However, it is amazing that in the Persian oral tradition, women were chosen as heroes back in ancient times, over thirty-five hundred years ago. This is evidence that during the time when there was no writing, and the spoken words were the only way of communication, there were heroes who were females. In the Farsi language or Persian, there is no gender identity in the third person singular or plural. So, there were no words such as "hero" or "heroine" for the creators of these stories to use. At the time when the storytellers developed these stories, very likely they wanted to show how a girl can be as brave or intelligent as a hero. Thus, they specifically called the stories, "The King and the Shepherd's Daughter," or "The Tailor's Daughter and the Chief Merchant's Son". Therefore, I take the liberty to use the word "hero" in place of "heroine" from now on.

It is clear that anyone is able to interpret the Persian folktales because of their archetypes. In addition, we can find out about the many varied traditions, beliefs, and other cultural situations of this nation through its folktales and fairytales. These seven tales, like any other stories are no exception. Persian beliefs, whether religious or superstitious, are distinctly depicted in this nation's tales.

This country was affected by two predominant religions—Zoroastrianism, the oldest religion, that precedes Judaism and Islam. In the latter, God's will is the main concern, and human life is predetermined by the Almighty. But in Zoroastrianism two powers, God (Ahura Mazda) and Evil (Ahriman), are in constant conflict within the person. Which wins out depends on man's behavior — when it is divine, the winner is Ahura Mazda and when it is devilish, it is Ahriman. In other words, the struggle of Good and Evil exists in one's mind. This conflict is depicted in all fairytales and folktales over and over throughout the different cultures.

Fazl-o'l-lah Mehtady, also known as Sobhi, a renowned storyteller, along with other scholars, strongly affirms that the Persian folktales and fairytales were altered under the influence of Arabs when they conquered Persia (651AD). Most of the earlier tales were destroyed because of their opposition to the Moslem beliefs and some others were changed to agree with the new religion. Sobhi points out:

The same way that the people became Moslem, they changed the stories according to their religion too. First, they started with names. [Roxana] was reversed to Fatima, just as [Afsheen to Ali]. In some places, they took out the word "book" or "notebook," and put the word 'Koran' instead. They changed Mobad (a Zoroastrian priest) to Molla (Moslem priest)....

Therefore, it is hardly possible to decide definitely which story belongs to the period before Islam or after it. These seven adventures clearly attest that the main theme in each one of them is still the conflict between good and evil, sometimes appearing in persons, animals, or between man and demon, or other supernatural creatures.

Interestingly all the Persian tales start with a sentence warning the audience about the strife between good and evil. The storyteller begins with *"yeki bood, yeki nabood ghair as khoda, hish kas nabood,"* which means, "There was one, there was no one, no one except God." This opening is full of conflicts. Hasan Mazloom in his article, "Research in Persian Folktales" explains that who is the "one" that exists and the other "one" who does not exist? Then the opening statement concludes with "...no one except God." If there was one why was there no one except God? And if the storyteller wants to say that the one was God Himself, then why does he deny this existence in "There was no one"? And when there was no one except God; then why does he tell us immediately about the character of the story that "There was a king who didn't have a son..." or "there was a poor wood-cutter..." and so on?

Each story also ends with the sentence, "Our story has come to an end; but the nightingale has not arrived home yet." As Mazloom continues to explain that the folktales are usually told during the nights while the nightingales are resting in their nests. But that is not important for the teller of stories. The main point is that he opens a long journey before this bird. And this fowl has never arrived home century after century and goes on hovering forever. At the end, each story hints to the theme that the bird of imagination never stops and keeps flying on and on. Thus, the storyteller shows with the beginning statement "There was one, there was no one…" and ends with the impossibilities of the nightingales ever reaching home. In other words, The storyteller tries to take away his audiences from the real world where time and place are two main elements which are limiting human life. He is eager to travel far to unlimited time and unknown places where magical events of the tales can happen.

Conflicts do not only exist in the beginning and the ending statements, but they also exist almost throughout the entire story. Each hero confronts the two contradicting poles in life such as beauty and ugliness, generosity and hypocrisy, goodness and wickedness. Even supernatural creatures are divided in two groups, some such as angels, who are good and pretty, and others such as demons, who are devilish and ugly. Five out of these seven stories depict clashes between these two forces in the life of each protagonist. The two exceptions are the Matron in "Yarrow—The Flower of Mother's Sweet Scent," and Neda in "The King and the Shepherd's Daughter." All the other characters must fight the devilish side of nature—the wicked aunts in "Brave Zara" and "The Story of Courageous Bibi," the vicious cousin, Goli in "The Tailor's Daughter and the Chief Merchant's Son," the mischievous sisters in "The Magic Reed," the thieves in "Brave Zara," and the three dangerous animals in "The Gardener and the Princess".

Ethics are integral to Persian tales. To serve the human race and to do good is the main lesson. In these stories, the benevolent act is always rewarded and devilish act is punished. The Moslem Persians believe that God rewards those who are kind and serve humanity, and punishes those who are malevolent to others. Zara is not chastised for causing Ahmad's death nor for beheading his friends because they are thieves and have diabolical intentions for Zara. Not only is she sanctified, but her daughter, Golnaz, is also blessed in her life; even though she, as an individual, must go through several challenges in her life until she is able to grasp happiness. Out of all the stories only the Matron in "Yarrow — the Flower of Mother's Sweet Scent," has no conflict, because she devotes her life to helping others. However, at the end she experiences anxiety in being separated from her daughter at the time of her death and makes it clear to her that she will be returning to her as a flower.

Fate or destiny is the foundation of Islam. The Iranian Moslems believe strongly that no-one has much power to control the events in her life. She is controlled by her fate, according to God's will. In other words, the Moslem belief is based on predestination. Whatever happens in life is pre-decided by God before birth, and there is no change whatsoever. Interestingly enough, in all of these stories, the heroes do not challenge whatever is predetermined for them. To their belief, for example, the shepherd's daughter, Neda's fate is to be smart enough to challenge the king and ultimately solves all the riddles presented to her. The same is true of Sahar, in "The Tailor's Daughter and the Chief Merchant's Son". However, Bibi's world in "The Story of Courageous Bibi," and Noor, in "The Magic Reed" deal with a magic and enchanting world. Moreover, the only time the main character remembers religion is in the time of difficulty when she seeks rescue in it. Golnaz's mother, Zara, calls on one of the Shi'ite-Moslem saints, the Saint Khizr, when she is in a difficult situation with Ahmad. Moreover, Bibi asks her husband's heinous aunt, Aafat, to give her some time to pray. The other heroes are not aware of religion or fate at all.

Similar to any other Persian stories, hope and happiness have a special place in these tales. As Mazloom indicates, Persians, like any other people, depict their own lost dreams in these stories. Usually at the end, the hero defeats the enemy, overcomes the problems, gets married to the princess and lives happily ever after. In these stories, six out of seven also ends with marriage — the unprivileged girl marries the prince, the chief-merchant's son or even the king. The hero achieves all that because of her courage, bravery and wits. Interestingly enough, only in "The Gardener and the Princess," Roxana, a princess, puts herself in danger, travels through the dark jungle to save her husband, who is not a royalty.

Any journey into the world of supernatural to save a marriage is also common in the Persian stories. In "The Story of Courageous Bibi," Bibi risks her life in order to rescue her husband from the wicked witch of Aafat. She takes her life in her hands and sets out on her odyssey. And because of all the upheavals she suffers, her mistake for not being honest to her husband and trusting Aafat instead, is forgiven and Aafat's spell is broken. In two other stories, "The King and the Shepherd's Daughter," and "The Tailor's Daughter and the Chief Merchant's Son," Neda and Sahar use their own wisdom rather than the supernatural to solve the riddles in order to reach happiness.

More of the Western stories end by male heroes getting married to their love and "…they live happily ever after." However, after considering these seven stories in this book, we understand that in five of them the challenges start right after their matrimony (which is not actually far from the truth of real life). These stories convey the idea that marriage is not an end but the beginning of a new life, especially for the bride. Like any other protagonist, she must go through some tests in order to be mature enough for starting a life with another person such as a king, a prince, or the head of the merchants.

Characters in Persian tales are typically Persian and universal as well. Mohammad J. Mahjoob describes the hero or protagonist in Persian tales as brave, good looking, noble and lovely. She never turns back from a conflict, and she is not discouraged by numerous problems. In other words, she never gives up, even after death, as in the case of Noor in "The Magic Reed".

In the oral tradition of any culture, the hero of the tale usually fights and rescues his lover whom he marries at the end. In these stories, some characters are also able to liberate their lovers. Bibi saves her husband from the devilish land of Aafat. The story goes on because of her love for Morad. In "The King and the Shepherd's Daughter," even though the king falls in love with the girl, he is not the one who undergoes testing. Neda must employ her intelligence to capture the king's respect and ultimately to be chosen to be the queen of Persia.

To consider the hero's adventure from the perspective of modern interpretation, most of the time Persian heroes go through three stages—

departure, initiation and return. In "The Magic Reed," the hero, Noor, transforms or departs into the different objects throughout her voyage until she completes her initiation stage. She dies when the lion eats her, but as a drop of blood she penetrates into the earth. After telling her story in the shape of a flute, she floats through the air as an ember, returning to the earth as a watermelon. Noor's journey is completed when she becomes mature enough to forgive her sisters. She realizes she has to have "wicked sisters" to grow to her utmost potential in life. She is not the only hero who goes through the three stages; four other heroes besides her in these tales go through several adventures and different experiences until they are able to fulfill their tasks and achieve their ultimate happiness.

The stories in this collection are originated in different regions of Iran and narrated by male storytellers based on their own imagination. All the seven stories are conceived from my Dissertation, *Land of Roses and Nightingales: A Collection and Study of Persian Folktales.* This study attests to Carl Jung's theory of "Collective Unconscious". In general, the Persian oral tradition upholds this theory to its best.

In the seven adventures, the narrator is the main character instead of a storyteller. Therefore, each hero is able to depict her story the way she sees it rather than to be manipulated by the storyteller's imagination.

These seven adventures are but a drop in the ocean of the Persian oral tradition, yet they stand the test of genuine folktales in their traditional styles and subjects while at the same time portraying how Persians, by choosing a female hero for their stories, were ahead of the rest of the ancient cultures, including the Greeks and the Romans. These odysseys of one girl fill a gap in world literature revealing that even in old times, peoples of this part of the world looked to women as equal to men.

By spreading the words of encouragement and education on life's contradictions, our youths can better learn how to rely on themselves; especially girls and young women. Consequently, each will act as a hero and can be triumphant on his or her own conflicts.

REFERENCES

Campbell, Joseph. *The Hero with a Thousand Faces.* Princeton: Princeton University Press, 1949.

Campbell, Joseph. *The hero's journey: Joseph Campbell on his life and work.* Vol. 7. New World Library, 1990.

Clouston, *William Alexander. A Group of Eastern Romances and Stories from the Persian, Tamil, and Urdu: With Introd., Notes, and App.* Privately Print. [Dr.]:(Hodge), 1889.

Eowyn Nelson, Elizabeth. *Psyche's Knife.* Wilmette, IL: Chiron Publications, 2012.

Idries Shah, Sayyid. *Tales of the Dervishes.* London: Cape Publications, 1967.

Jung, C.G. *Four Archetypes: Mother/Rebirth/Spirit/Trickster.* Translated by R.F.C. Hull. Princeton: Princeton University Press, 1959.

Jung, C.G. *Jung to Live by.* New Haven, CT: Yale University Press, 1973.

Jung, C.G. *Man and His Symbols.* New York: Dell Publishing Co., 1964.

Jung, C.G. *The Undiscovered Self with Symbols and the Interpretation of Dreams.* Translated by R.F.C. Hull. Princeton: Princeton University Press, 1990.

Mahjoob, Mohammad J. ["A Study in Iranian Folktales"]. *Ketabe Hafte* 84, [June 1963]: 108.

Mazloon, Hasan. ["A Research in Iranian Folktales"]. *Talash* 10, [October 1967]: 18.

Mehtady (Sobhi), F. [The Influence of Iranian Tales on Foreign Tales.] *Mardomshenasi* 2 [July 1958]:119-121.

Mehtady 9Sobhi), F. *Afsane-Haye-Kohan* [The Ancient Iranian Tales] Tehran: Amir Kabir Co., [1970].

Pinkola Estes, Clarissa. *Women Who Run with Wolves.* New York: Ballantine Books, 1992.

READER'S GUIDE

- What themes were most memorable for you throughout the tales? Describe.

- What word, sentence, or image captures how you felt after reading this book?

- What events or characters in any of the tales resonate with your life?

- What are some differences between the Persian girl and a modern girl in Western Society? Similarities?

- What heroic characteristics in the Persian girl stand out for you? Why?

- Were there times the Persian girl's courage wavered? Why?

- Do you think in any of the seven adventures, the Persian girl changes? How?

- Discuss the religion role in every tale.

- What surprised you most in reading this collection of fairytales?

- What did you learn about Persian culture?

CPSIA information can be obtained
at www.ICGtesting.com
Printed in the USA
BVHW02*0119080718
520866BV00001B/1/P

9 781732 067714